Thomas I. Wharton

A Latter Day Saint

being the story of the conversion of Ethel Jones related by herself

Thomas I. Wharton

A Latter Day Saint
being the story of the conversion of Ethel Jones related by herself

ISBN/EAN: 9783337335786

Printed in Europe, USA, Canada, Australia, Japan

Cover: Foto ©Andreas Hilbeck / pixelio.de

More available books at **www.hansebooks.com**

A LATTER DAY SAINT

BEING THE STORY

OF THE CONVERSION OF ETHEL JONES

RELATED BY HERSELF

NEW YORK
HENRY HOLT AND COMPANY
1884

W. L. Mershon & Co.,
Printers and Electrotypers,
Rahway, N. J.

A LATTER DAY SAINT.

I.

I MUST lightly indicate my early history. My father was a prosperous business man in the city of Philadelphia. No name on Market street was more respected, and certainly no store front on Market street was uglier, than his. He was a kindly man, entirely devoted to his business, and all the more because it demanded a slight knowledge of science, which gave him an excuse for subscribing to the *Scientific American* and forming cabinets of "specimens." I was exceedingly fond of him, and he, I think, preferred me to my younger sister, who was a prig, as many little girls are. It may be that I ought to ascribe my father's preference to the fact that, being a precocious child, I soon learned how to play at billiards, for it was in that game that he found his chief, and indeed his only, relaxation. In course of time I became quite an adept, though it was tiresome to have to knock the balls about night after night; and many a long evening have I spent in my father's company stretching myself across our big green table and chalking my tall cue with childish gravity. My mother was as ambitious as my father was contented. Long before either of her daughters was old enough to understand the meaning of the word " position " she had discovered that it was impossible to convey to his mind in any way the idea that there could be any thing wanting to ours. His idea for the future happiness of Ethel and Elizabeth Jones was that we were to marry energetic young business men, live quietly in the country, and raise peas and families to be the admiration and despair of our neighbors. It may be imagined that my mother rarely endeavored to convince him how trite were his ideas when I add that whenever these visions of the future pastoral happiness of his daughters presented themselves to his mind he invariably was excited to declare an intention to retire from business himself and taste similar bucolic joys on my grandfather's farm in Lancaster county. My mother's hopes, however, were none the less distinct because my father did not happen to share in them ; she looked to us for a double share of energy and pains. One at least of her daughters has not disappointed her.

My mother was an ignorant woman in many ways, but she was quick, appreciative, far-sighted, and possessed of considerable knowledge of the world—or, rather, of the failings of the world, which amounts to the same thing. It was this knowledge that enabled her to succeed in establishing relations with advantageous people against the time of our growing up. Considering her disadvantages (for she never dared to allow my father to suspect that she was intriguing for her daughters) her success was wonderful. Perhaps the success she did obtain was not so wonderful as her tact and self-control. She managed never to appear pushing, she always behaved with good taste, and she kept several obnoxious relations out of the way ; but as I incline to think, after my father's failure and death, all her care might have been of no avail whatever. Old Mr. Latitude told her that she would have a doosid hard time to get those girls into Philadelphia society—and his reasons for saying so were excellent.   He also desired her to count on him for assistance ; but as his function in society was simply the collation, condensation, and diffusion of gossip, his offer involved more temporary good will on his part than future profit to my mother.   It certainly looked as if she were going to have a hard time, and we might easily have dropped out of sight, for though we had acquaintance with some people it rested with us to keep it up ; and I was only fifteen. I am inclined to ascribe our success to the fact that my mother was able to keep us at Miss Mayburn's school.   It helped matters to a certain extent that my mother immediately crossed the Rubicon of Market street and estab-

lished herself among the people whom we wished
to know, but we might never have accomplished
any thing further if it had not been for the con-
nections we were able to form at Miss Mayburn's, and the kindness of the girls we met
there. We were not entirely unknown, to be
sure, nor altogether disapproved of, when we
first went there. My mother has often reminded me of her policy with Mrs. Hathorne at
Cape May. It was our first visit to the sea—
we had been used to spend our summers at my
grandfather's farm—and before Mrs. Hathorne
appeared we had been allowed to run wild with
some children whose manners were not too bad,
but whose voices and appearance were of Pitts-
burgh, Pittsburghy; and I imagine that we were
at times disagreeable. But when Lotty and
Gerty Hathorne appeared our liberties were
snatched from us. On the beach we were at-
tended by my mother's maid, and my mother in
the meantime waited three days for another
servant; our dinners we took no longer in the
public dining hall, but at the nurse's and

children's table; the fine muslins and broad sashes in which we had delighted were laid aside, and we soberly wore our flannel dresses all day long. My mother took care to behave in Mrs. Hathorne's presence as if they had exchanged positions; and the consequence was that at the end of the week we were familiar with the girls and Mrs. Hathorne had conversed amicably with my mother upon the beach. I do not think, therefore, that Mrs. Hathorne was greatly displeased some one or two years afterwards to find that Lotty and I were in the same class at Miss Mayburn's, and very likely to become intimate. I look back to my school days with gratitude, affection and regret. According to my father's preconceived notions we ought to have been sent to a boarding school; but he was unable to make up his mind to exile us from home, and he made no objection to our going to Miss Mayburn, especially as her's was supposed to be the best girls' school in town. With my mother, of course, it was a matter of calculation; for at that time nearly

all the girls whom it was most important for me
to know were of Miss Mayburn's flock. I think
the five years that I spent under her care were
the happiest, in many ways, that I have ever
known. To be sure, while I was there, my
father died, and for some time I was deeply
afflicted; moreover, during the last three years,
that is, from the time of my father's death until
the end of my school days, I was conscious that
my object at school should be to gain something more than an education. Yet I was ambitious enough to overlook my own insincerity,
and fond enough of my friends to be glad to
try to bind them closer to me, and—I confess it
—not even the flush of my greatest triumphs
has been so grateful to me as was the friendship
and, when I had it, the approbation of Miss
Mayburn. How we all feared and worshiped
her! How we all admired her strength and
vigor, her wonderful culture and forgetfulness
of self, her keen sympathy and quick humor!
She was born to cheer and instruct her own
sex, not for the benefit, except indirectly, of

man.   For my own part she imbued me with a
fondness for literature which was not wholly
native to me, and tightened the cords of my
resolution by the force of her decided example.
But I never copied her handwriting as most of
the girls did.   It was at Miss Mayburn's school,
then, that I laid the foundations of my success.
My mother was one of the first to send her
daughters to that school in order to get them
into society, but I was probably as successful as any girl that ever tried the plan.
Some girls, either from incompetence or pride,
have graduated as unknown as they were when
first they hung their flaxen heads and pulled at
their dresses in the awful presence of Miss Mayburn.   My success was complete.   Lotty
Hathorne became my most intimate friend, and
as the girls in my class grew up I was recognized as a member of the little set that led the
school.   I could draw caricatures, I could write
passable rhymes, I was the leader of the consol-
idated-recess party, when that memorable con-
troversy agitated our class.   Miss Mayburn in

our last year had proposed to allow us to take only quarter hour recesses throughout the week and as an offset to leave school an hour earlier on Fridays; and when the girls hesitated I formed a party, suggested the maneuver of obtaining significant and ominous certificates from medical experts (some of the girls' fathers gave us delightful opinions,) argued the question before the class in several stormy recesses, and won our case. When we acted, I was always stage manager; when we had our orgies I was generally chosen Toast Mistress, an office which was equivalent to being an executive committee to get Miss Mayburn's permission to buy the cake, the cream chocolates and the lemons, and to keep the girls from snatching. Sometimes we did have toasts—I always made poor Olive Grene respond to the toast of The Gentlemen because Willy Woodburn walked to school with her three mornings out of the week, leaving her at the corner. Thus I became intimate with the other girls, they confided to me their little secrets, I came to know all about their boyish admirers, and, for the matter of that, heard the name of more than one older man, I drew sly little pictures representing scenes from real life (which were sources of infinite delight to my companions), and, in short, when we graduated, I was as much one of them as if their mothers had speculated with mine over our respective cradles as to our probable friendships and destinies. I had never been to a party, I knew absolutely no men at all, I had only been to the houses of my friends' mammas in the afternoon and on evenings when no one else was present— and this for several reasons, chiefly that I had been for a long time in mourning, that I really had to drudge laboriously to help my mother with her slender housekeeping, and that in those days also I was ambitious enough to work very hard at my books,—but I looked forward with agreeable certainty to going out more and more until at last no door should be closed to me. I counted on my friends, and I was not mistaken. I am most profoundly grateful to them.

To be sure, I amused them ; but their kindness none the less calls for my gratitude. My schooling at Miss Mayburn's had done the trick, as Mr. Latitude truthfully remarked to my mother. Without it, I should have had to depend on chance, and all the more so because I was not at the time particularly pretty. I was considered very pretty during my second winter when my figure had become graceful ; but now I had only my complexion and my eyes. When I think of my complexion ! I had the most delicate soft brown skin, and the little tinge on my cheeks was not incorrectly spoken of, perhaps, by some of my admirers, as the most exquisite thing imaginable. Be it understood that I am speaking of departed glories. My eyes, thank heaven, I still possess, but my hair, or some of it, has gone into rats.

I have said that I knew absolutely no men. Let me qualify the statement. I knew one or two boys, some college youths and—Mr. Branscombe Boullter. Bran Boullter I shall always consider the most fascinating man I ever saw.

From my earliest days—I mean, of course, my earliest enlightened days—I had heard of him as *the* man with whom it was necessary for a girl to spar a little before she could consider her education in the noble art of self-defense complete. My sex ought to rejoice that he strictly conformed to the bachelor faith. I had seen him over and again, 1 had depicted him in all kinds of attitudes, I had wedded his name to immortal verse—and when he began to be attentive to Lotty Hathorne, I made up my mind that I was going to profit by it. He began to be attentive to Lotty in the winter of our last year at school, which was a little early; for, though he usually looked over the buds of each year in the spring before they came out, he rarely took much notice of them before they appeared in their Easter bravery.. But at whatever time he applied himself he was sure of success. Often did Neddy Tryffleham experience the galling pang of seeing a girl whom he had carefully worked up while she was yet in her bread-and-butter days, snatched away from

him before his very eyes by Bran the Irresist-
ible. Mr. Boullter was quite impecunious, every
body knew he was not serious, and there was
not a girl in town who did not adore him and
long to play at believing in him. My satisfaction, then, can well be imagined when one day
Mr. Boullter took it into his head that he sufficiently desired to speak to Lotty to stride after
her in the street as she was walking with me and
to join us both with a gay air that proclaimed that
he didn't care whether he knew me or not. Of
course Lotty presented him to me, and I walked
along on the inside, greatly triumphing, and to
my surprise, perfectly cool. He had on a gray
walking coat, rough and loose ; his trousers were
gray and of elegant cut, and it seemed to me then
as if there was something almost divine in the
way his collar and cravat harmonized with his
sun-burned neck and crisp golden hair. He
naturally directed most of his conversation to
Lotty, and at intervals only slipped in a word
to me. When we reached her door-step there
was a halt.

I could not go in, and Mr. Boullter declined Lotty's invitation to lunch. We had met him going in the opposite direction, and though I knew that his concern was only with Lotty, just as he was preparing to pretend to leave me with her I looked at him. He afterwards declared that I gave him a broadside " that raked me fore and aft, I assure you, Miss Ethel!" but at the time he behaved with great coolness, merely remarking, as if he had intended to say it all the time, "And if Miss Jones will permit me, I will escort her home. I am going to my office, I protest, and it won't take me at all out of my way." I wanted horribly to wink at Lotty, but was afraid to do so, so I walked off without throwing my umbrella up in the air or indulging in any expressions of triumph.

He was actually by my side, my property for the time being; on me those eyes were bent, to me that adorable voice spoke. He was just a trifle more interested than he had been, but I was rather calm. I knew that this walk was only tentative. He talked easily about having heard of me from my friend Miss Hathorne, hinted that he understood that I was clever at my pen, and said he hoped to see me next winter.

"I don't think it likely that I shall go out much, Mr. Boullter," said I. I went on immediately, (for I didn't want him to think I was "fishing"). "A young person who is possessed of talents remarkable as mine are, according to your account, had better occupy herself in cultivating them rather than in—"

"Now don't blackguard society before you see it," said Bran, interrupting me, "it's quite a jolly place, you know."

"I am very fond of my books, however," I answered.

"The proper study of womankind is man," said he. Then he began to smile. "If you prefer to study the individual rather than the race, I shall be very happy to give you object lessons."

"I think," said I, "that I should prefer to

begin with race characteristics. Then I could better understand the individual."

"I fancy," said he, "that you understand both pretty well."

I am free to say that I think I did. I knew instinctively that it would be commonplace to ask him to be good to me if I did go out; I knew that I couldn't make him want to do so by asking him point blank to do it, or by letting him see that I had led up the conversation to making him offer to do it; and I felt that the true way to encourage him was to refuse his advances by word of mouth and accept them by word of eye.

"Thank you for the compliment," said I. "In return for which I shall have to accept your offer of the object lessons—on condition that you let me choose the object."

"Certainly," he replied, "I should not care, myself, to be the object."

"Ah?" said I. I came terribly near being afraid that he was piqued, and hastening to say that I wished him to be the object, for I did not foresee a quibble.

" Because," he went on, " I should prefer to
be—a—your subject, you know." The pun was
not good, even for a pun, but it certainly pleased
me ; and the killing little way in which he said
" your *subject* " quite overcame me. Luckily
for my presence of mind our door was just at
hand, and I could ask him to ring the bell.
Goodness! how victorious I felt. Unless my
unpracticed eyes deceived me, *he wanted me to
ask him to come in !* But I did not do so, and
as he held out his hand, (it was unnecessary, to
be sure, but I *had* made eyes at him,) he said :

" When I next come this way I hope that it
may be—"

" With an object," said I, finishing the sentence for him with as much calmness as possible.

My delight was only natural ; and my rest
was disturbed that night by dazzling visions of
future successes and glories. My anticipations
had formerly been somewhat vague, but that
day I felt the full force of a material, distinct
desire. I wanted to know every man in town

so that I might vanquish each one in turn if possible—and I wanted, oh how I wanted to get into the full swing of pleasure and *go it !* That familiar if vulgar phrase exactly expresses what I meant ; and I determined that when I got the chance I *would* " go it," and I think that before I finally stopped building air-castles and dropped off to sleep, I added, " and with a vengeance ! "

The chance to know more men arrived sooner than I had expected.

Lotty had been permitted by her mother, in anticipation of her going out, to fill their country house with young people for a week in the end of June, and the dear girl immediately wrote to say that she must of course have me. " As you may imagine, Ethel," she said, "you and I are to be the *Not-outs of the team.*" " A certain person," she continued, " may be angry if he likes, but he is only a *boy*, even if he *is* at college, and *I shall not ask him.* Did I tell you how *furious* he was when I informed him that we had been reading Juvenal. He said that he

knew we couldn't do it, and at any rate it wasn't
fit reading for us, and that he wondered *how*
Miss Mayburn could *give* it to us. You may
imagine that I did not tell him that it was only
twenty lines, and that Miss Mayburn had to
read them to us after all."

It was rather ruthless in Lotty to ask only
the older men and pass over her younger admirers, but I was very glad she did so, and
profited accordingly. What a jolly time we
had! For a really consistently perfect time
commend me to a well-stocked country-house
in summer. It was my first glimpse of Society-
Canaan, and I saw it, not from a height, but
face to face. How pleasant it was to sit on a
rug, under the trees, and talk nonsense in the
gayest of manners; how delightful to have
lying at your feet a bronzed and whiskered
cavalier, who dealt out to you easy compliment and polite insinuation as if it was your
hereditary due; how charming the freedom, the
merry-making, the songs, the romps, the little
understandings, the little private jokes! I could

hardly take my eyes off the men. It was so interesting to watch their free movements, to see them put their big hands on each other's shoulders, light their pipes, touch off fireworks with their cigars, help the girls across brooks, twirl their whiskers—to hear their deep voices and put one's hand through their hard, their awfully hard, strong arms. Even to notice their ways at dinner was absorbing, and I took a positive pleasure in seeing them drink sangaree or ale in the mornings after playing tennis. (That was the first year that lawn tennis was played, the Hathornes being almost the first people to have a set, and the men were wonderfully keen about it.) They seemed to reciprocate my feelings. Lotty used to tell me every night, while we brushed out our hair, of some new nice thing that a man had said about me. If I had believed that deceitful wretch, Bran Boullter, I should have ended my days in an insane asylum, for my brain would have been turned by a delusion of vanity. He spent a good deal of time with me during that blissful week—he was one of the two or three men who staid all the time—and, although he was really more attentive to Lotty, and probably at that time liked her better, I came in for his best manner and his most charming guile. Well, I played accompaniments, and was as agreeable as Punch to every body, and didn't take advantage of being Lotty's friend, and didn't show temper—and was, in short, as careful as any girl could well have been, and I think I deserved to be liked. At first I came very near using my eyes too much, but stopped myself in time.

After that Lotty asked me to stay some time with her, but I thought it better not to run the risk of tiring my hosts, so I only staid a day after the others went, in order to make a good impression on Mrs. Hathorne, and then I returned triumphant to my mother. I believe my mother would have viewed with absolute satisfaction the prospect of working herself to a skeleton in order to advance her daughters' social welfare. She took an almost absurd delight in my tales, and tried my patience, if the truth must be told, by asking me thousands of repeated questions. I was rather self-sufficient, just then, and preferred to treat every thing that occurred to me as the most natural thing in the world and beneath discussion.

That summer was spent in quiet at my grandfather's farm. I almost had a fit of crying when my mother produced, (this was before we left Philadelphia), a little sum of money that she had put away for me, which she gave me, with tears in her eyes and a half-framed blessing, telling me it was for my dresses next winter. We did a certain amount of shopping in town, and sewed a good deal while we were at Lancaster. My grandfather, too, bless his dear soul, gave me a handsome "tip," as the boys call it; and many a pleasant afternoon did my mother and I spend together over my dresses, she dwelling with a good deal of spirit and color of language on the good luck she anticipated for me, I elaborating, with a little consciousness of my own cleverness, my theories of life and society—which were already pretty well formed. I had by this time recovered from the sobering effect of Miss Mayburn's last words to me when I went through the time-honored ceremony of a farewell interview with her before leaving school for ever. They were words that I half expected to hear yet half hoped not to hear. I know now why she did not give me the praise which I secretly thought was my due; I know now why she tried to make me see that life was not a bed of roses; but at the time I hardly cared to have her tell me that only hard work and an abiding faith could bring happiness in this world. The strong faced and dignified woman sat by the table in her little study in the attitude which all her girls know so well—with one foot pushed forward, her arm on the table, her hand stroking her smooth hair and her other hand lying in her lap—looking at me intently. "Ethel," she said, "no woman can be thoroughly good or thoroughly happy who is not really a religious woman." I returned her gaze. I heard, but I think that I knew I was going to forget.

II.

WHEN we returned to town in the middle of September I was "all agog to dash through thick and thin," and all the more impatient because I knew that two months must yet elapse before the season would fairly begin. A visit to Lotty when her family came home from Newport and Olive Grene's garden party helped to stay my desires to a small extent; and, as every week passed by, I used to see one or two of the men whom by that time I knew strolling through Rittenhouse square or walking in Walnut street. Mr. Boullter insisted on rowing me up the river. I think he would willingly have had me take supper with him at Strawberry Mansion quite by ourselves, but I positively refused to row with him alone except in the morning; and I only did it once, being a little disturbed, I confess, by the other men at the boat house. Not that I was afraid of them;

I did not want to be talked about, and at that time did not know enough to discriminate. I would gladly have been rowed by him for days together, however, for he looked admirable in flannels.

At last came the great event—Mrs. Hathorne's dinner for Lotty.

I feel again my thrill of delight on hearing our door-bell ring as I stood in my room on that well-remembered evening, for I knew that it must be Olive Grene, who had promised to come for me in her coupé. I scarcely waited for the little maid to tell me that the carriage had come, but kissed my mother affectionately, gave a peck at my sister Bessy, who had been bothering me a good deal with persistent questions and suggestions, and flew down-stairs in order to escape any family demonstration on the doorstep. I found Olive in quite a whirl of excitement. Her wildness infected me, and when we rustled in from the dark street to the blazing hall at the Hathornes' I felt almost ready to rush into the little ante-room, through the half

open door of which I caught a glimpse of
masculine figures and heard a snatch of masculine laughter, execute a fandango and dance
out again, just by way of prelude to the
evening's diversion. But I was sobered by
suddenly finding myself in Lotty's room, face
to face with two or three girls whom I did not
know, and with Letty Risquict, who instantly
tried to snub me ; and my thoughts were turned
to the graver aspect of the situation. I threw
off my cloak and carefully inspected myself,
and then hastened to the assistance of Olive,
who had misplaced a ribbon or lost a pin ; and
presently we went down to the parlor, where
stood Mrs. Hathorne, calm and gracious, and
Lotty, who was looking very pretty and a little
flushed. The men were all on the field before
us; and in a very short time we had formed
our procession, and were parading into the
dining-room. I was taken in by Mr. Mason
Temple, as I had expected. Indeed, when
Lotty offered me my choice among the men,
I determined upon him. I longed for Mr.

Boullter, it is true, but I did not dare to ask
for him; and I remembered that when Mr.
Temple saw me sitting on a haycock at the
Grene's garden-party, he told Olive that I made
the prettiest Phyllis he had ever beheld, and
so I named him for my Amintor. When I
announced my determination to Lotty, she
said that as I had declared for sentiment, she
would see that I did not lose any worldly advantage; and that she would put Mr. Charter
on the other side of me. "Macy" Temple, as
every body called him, was a tall, slight young
man, with a good humored expression, who
made fun of himself when nobody else could
be found for a victim, who was something of a
dilettante, and supposed to be a contributor to
the magazines; Mr. Algernon Fairfax Van
Strouslaer Penn Charter (his mother had been
one of the Van Strouslaers, and *her* mother a
Fairfax—) possessed a pedigree before which
Englishmen might have bowed, and gymnastic
ability which was said to be the delight of pro-
fessionals—in addition to which he was of con-

siderable fortune, very fond of entertaining, and, as he was accustomed to call himself, "a well-known sport!" Between these two young men I felt eminently well satisfied, and, to my surprise, perfectly calm. I looked around the table as I drew off my gloves. It was a large dinner—twenty-six, I think—and Lotty had made it up very carefully. It was supposed to contain the choicest of the men in society, and the most promising of the buds of the season. It was quite a distance from one end of the long table to the other, and the room looked magnificent with its high walls covered with family portraits, and this splendid glittering parallelogram in the very middle under the chandelier. I looked down the row of faces; everybody was talking and laughing—there was a rattle of conversation. I laughed softly to myself, and drummed on the table. The cloth was deliciously white; my fingers looked so smooth and clean and delicate that I quite fell in love with them. The plate before me was Sévres; a lovely basket of Jacqueminot roses

was placed in front of it; any number of bewildering wine-glasses, some cut glass, some
Bohemian, stood at hand; the silver was King
pattern. Further off was a gorgeous épergne,
round the corner of which I could see Olive
smiling at me; I drew a long breath in the
fullness of my joy, and, as Mr. Temple was
looking away, I turned to Mr. Charter and
beamed upon him. His face lighted up in a
remarkably sudden manner, and he gently took
my dinner card, which I had been twiddling in
my fingers, and proposed to draw a diagram of
the table on it for me. He took up a tiny gold
champagne bottle which dangled from his
watch-chain, out of which he shot a little pen-
cil—and then, before beginning his task, and
as if with a fresh access of hope, begged me to
exchange my dinner card for his. Mr. Temple,
who had by this time turned round, objected
strongly to Mr. Charter's plans; and of course
the latter persisted, though he ought to have
been attending to his own girl. They both
appealed to me so violently, that I was a little

afraid of making a mistake, and felt for a moment that it would be better to keep my card as a safe method of settling the dispute, but I quickly recovered myself, and bade Mr. Temple remember that he had taken his eyes off me, and naturally ought to suffer for it. Mr. Charter accordingly kept my card, and began writing the names of the party for me on his own, a labor much interrupted by scornful remarks from Mr. Temple, who, I instantly saw, could be very amusing if he wished. In the course of time Mr. Charter finished the card and presented it to me with an air of triumph; but his face fell when I allowed Mr. Temple to persuade me to accept his *boutonnière*, and give him one of my roses in place of it. Up to this time I had felt a little that I ought not to encourage another girl's man *too* much; but my conscience hardened with my success, especially as Mr. Charter had taken in Letty Risquict, to whom I owed a grudge for her behavior to me in the dressing-room, and I now laid myself out to keep both men talking to me as long as

possible, so I smiled at all Mr. Charter's some
what glaring compliments, I capped Mr.
Temple's quotations, I shook my head with a
look that might have meant any thing at the
insinuations of each about the other; till,
finally (but not until the Roman punch came
round) Mr. Charter found that his staying
powers were not so good as those of his adver-
sary, and turned to Letty with a somewhat
guilty look. She, as I hoped, and subsequently
was assured, was angry enough to have upset
the salad-dressing over me.

As Mr. Charter turned away, Mr. Temple
gave vent to a prodigious sigh of pretended
relief. " At last I have you to myself," said he.

" But you have been talking to me all the
evening," I answered.

" Mr. Charter has been listening to me, too."

" Do you grudge me the attention of another
man ? Oh, how selfish is your sex ! "

" Rather, how grasping is your's ! You have
made me wait till now for an opportunity to say
what you know I have been dying to say to you."

As he murmured these last words his face
wore an expression of the most intense earnest-
ness—but there was a twinkle in the corner of
his eye. I determined that if he was going to
be outrageous I would be outrageous too.

"Perhaps," I said, with an air of diffidence,
"perhaps I was afraid to listen to you."

I saw that he would have liked to laugh, but
did not wish to spoil the flirtation.

"May I say it," he whispered again, in pas-
sionate tones.

I pretended to look at my fan, and then
turned round to him. "Yes," I said.

He pretended to hesitate. "And yet I dare
not, so soon," he said. Then he began to
repeat—

> " ' Si vous croyez que je vais dire
> Qui j'ose aimer,
> Je ne saurais pour un empire
> Vous la nommer !' "

I was staggered by this; I had not expected
him to be indirect. I laid down my fork and
looked at him with mock agitation. "Oh, be

explicit!" I cried. "Do not fear! let me encourage you!"

A slight smile flickered round his lips for a
moment. Then his face grew grave and he
said in a low tone, "Heavens! how beautiful
your eyes are!"

I was caught. I blushed—faltered—I had
to surrender. I laughed till I blushed again
for laughing, and then laughed for blushing
again.

After this our flirtation had to stop altogether
or take a more really serious turn. I shall leave
the reader to imagine upon which course we
decided. I am very glad that Mr. Temple was
not mischievous, for I might easily have been
induced to disgrace myself. He was sufficiently
to blame for making me flirt with him as wildly
as I did—though, after all, it made very little
difference, for every girl at the table was almost
as excited as I was myself. When the crackers
were being pulled I looked round again—my
first general glance since the beginning of dinner. Every body was talking at once; private

3

raids were being made upon the dishes of fruit and sweetmeats—a candle fell down in front of Mr. Boullter, who picked it up, relighted it and quietly fixed it upon the plate of the girl next to him, whereupon the man on the other side of her blew it out; the girl herself laughing and expostulating with both of them.

But now, much to my disgust, Mrs. Hathorne rose to lead us girls from the room. I followed her with a sigh, which Mr. Temple, in choking tones, immediately declared he echoed. He had previously, during the course of the dinner, much deplored the custom which made men remain at table after the women went to the parlor, but declared that he had not the moral courage to break through it. As we edged slowly towards the door I offered him another rose from my basket if he would accompany me to the parlor on this occasion, but he said that he wouldn't dare to offend the other men and that his doctor had ordered him to smoke " for a cruel nervous disease." I came very near telling him that I wished I could stay with him; and, indeed, I did wish to do so most violently, this desire being much stronger than the conflicting desire to go and talk it over with the girls, for I knew fairly well what *they* would say, and I positively ached to hear the male comments on the dinner; and I had a feeling that I should like to try a cigarette.

When the girls got together again in the parlor there was a buzz of "my dears;" but, after a minute or two, we began to adjust ribbons and laces and to commend each other's appearance. This necessary duty being over we began once more to talk over our fellow-men. Olive Grene broke away from a little knot of girls and rushed toward me. "Girls," she cried out, "did you ever see any thing so barefaced as Ethel's flirting?" Several of my friends made a group about me, and for a moment or two I was a target for all manner of accusations, till I was able to restrain my choking laughter and retaliate in kind. Milly Mortmain caused much excitement by declaring that she had extracted from an anonymous man at the dancing

class the night before, an opinion about every
girl in society; but as, when she was met by
the immediate question: "Oh, Milly! what
did he say about me?" she vowed that she was
bound to secrecy, it was generally allowed that
she was endeavoring to hoax us; for of course
no girl would hesitate to break such a promise
as that. By the time we had finished our cof-
fee I know I was quite ready for the men to
join us, and I fancy that most of the girls felt as
I did; but we were forced to wait for some time,
while every now and then we heard the most
tantalizing bursts of laughter from below. At
last they appeared, Mr. Temple leading the
way. I expected him to make for my side, but
it seemed understood that the men were to
talk no more to their partners at the table, but
were to devote themselves to other girls. Just
as I began to fancy that Bran Boullter was
looking in my direction, a tall distinguished-
looking man who had been presented to me before dinner, and whom I had some difficulty in
remembering as Mr. Middleton Hall, came up

to me. He bowed with a grave elegance of manner, and began at once, not a little to my surprise, to speak to me of my father, whom he said he remembered with feelings of great respect and gratitude. He explained to me the reason; it was only, I think, that about the time when he was admitted to the bar he made a great blunder through which a very important case in which my father was interested was nearly lost, and that my father instead of being very angry treated him with much kindness and patience. I confess that this conversation of Mr. Hall's jarred on me. The topic was quite at variance with my lively mood, and when Mr. Hall spoke of my father I could not help feeling slightly conscious. But though Mr. Hall's presence was somewhat irksome to me at first, I found myself, after some time, becoming interested in his conversation. He began by asking me, but without any of the customary affectation, how I liked going about, and then, instead of annoying me with stale compliments and threadbare prophesies, talked very sensibly and very well about the necessity for social intercourse and the impropriety of judging the aims and effects of society by the internal feelings of pleasure or disappointment experienced by any member of it. "If," said he, "we are called upon to decide between the fanatic hermit and the empty-headed fop, we are apt to declare in favor of the former, since his actions appear to us at least to be grounded upon reflection; yet in many cases we might find the hermit was actuated only by the sting of disappointment, the sway of avarice, the suggestions of spite and resentment, or the inability to conquer some morbid physical propensity—and that he possessed, no more than the fashionable butterfly, a logical conclusion by which to justify his habits and actions. I don't mean to say," said he, smiling, "that I think a fop the most admirable object in nature, but I'm not sure that he deserves all the abuse heaped upon him. And I dare say a misanthropist might just as well cloak his feelings under the disguise of folly as proclaim them in the character of a hermit."

He said a good deal more, to which I listened intently, feeling quite sorry to have him go when he rose to leave me, and I stopped him eagerly when he began to apologize for the dryness of his conversation. As he moved away, a voice behind me said :

"I will answer for Mr. Hall's dreams to-night."

I turned to behold Bran Boullter leaning towards me. I need not repeat what he said. It was the second time that evening that I had been complimented on my eyes. Some of the girls were by this time going off to a small dance at Leila Girard's, but Lotty begged the rest of us to stay, and so we gathered together round the little tea-table, and Lotty made us all take a second cup of tea. What a jolly hour we spent together! Bran Boullter and Mason Temple were more amusing than I had ever imagined any body could be; and though I afterwards discovered the innate spitefulness of that little wretch Hamelin Towne, at that time I could not but be delighted with his descrip-

tions of people and his mimicry. It was twelve
o'clock before we got away. Bran Boullter
and Mason Temple put us into the carriage,
and Bran gave my hand an exceedingly affectionate squeeze as he said good-by—and I'm not
sure that I didn't return it. As we rattled up
the street—of course Mrs. Grene's coupè was
not built to be run on the car tracks—I grasped
Olive's hand and said :

"Hasn't it been just too perfect for any
thing!"

"Goodness, yes!" she answered. "I could
dine forever!"

III.

THUS were the gates of social paradise opened; and thus did the Peri enter in. But in a short time the Peri discovered that she was not entirely happy. It is a fact; I was not satisfied. For I had determined not to be careless enough to presume upon the Hathorne patronage. I knew that the stamp of Mrs. Hathorne's approval would enable me to pass current, but I wanted to be at a premium on my own account. I sacrificed myself on the altar of character. Never did I knowingly offend any body; never did I indulge myself in any of those little sarcasms to inflict which on some of my female acquaintance my tongue at times fairly ached. The mammas and maiden aunts in Congress assembled must have voted that I was fresh milk and pure Canaan honey —a model and a delight. From Miss Mayburn and Mr. Temple I obtained quite a character for cleverness; but I never allowed myself to outshine other folk, unless I was talking to some body who would detect politic restraint on my part. Macy Temple, though he always assumed that dreadful and wildly aggravating masculine tone of superiority, and spoke as if he had concluded to exhibit the truth to his female friends, but to suffer in silence if they offended against it, was never jealous of other people's talents, and took care that no one should estimate my abilities at a lower value than he himself had decided to put on them. He often did me the honor to bring me little poems and literary sketches of which he made a great secret; and he sometimes did me the much greater honor to beg for my opinion. We became great friends; he told me what Miss Mayburn had said to him about the character of my mind, and pointed out to me what he considered the mistakes in her estimate; he suggested several courses of reading for me, and took a most kindly interest in my intellectual welfare. But let nobody suppose that he was an æsthete.

He discovered no signs of æstheticism in the composition of bouquets; if he preferred sun-flowers to jacqueminots, he took very good care to hide his taste when he wished to compliment me; and though he was very well up in the stained-glass poets and nearly made me weep by reading to me " Sir Peter Harpdon's End," I don't think he cared as much for Perugino or Botticelli as he did for the cartoons in Puck. Whenever we indulged in an occasional bit of flirtation I could not help thinking of Mr. Boullter, with whom very few men compared favorably. I must do Mr. Temple the justice to say that in his own way he was charming. He had a very attractive way of hinting com-pliments, entrapping you in a pleasing pitfall of compliment to which he would lead you care-fully through ways of apparently barren com-monplace. But he was not sufficiently exciting. His method was too coldly intellectual; there was not enough warmth about his style nor *soupçon* of danger in his glance.

Then, too, I did not care to see too much of

him, for I thought it best not to be supposed
to be intimate with any man during my first
winter; and as he was accustomed to having
his own way he was displeased at being frequently put off. For the same reason I took care
not to encourage Mr. Boullter too much; in a
word, my policy was to bring all the men to my
side but not to keep any of them there too long.

And oh, heavens! when I remember the
ennui which I endured during the sessions of
those awful sewing classes and Bible classes
which I servilely joined when invited so to do,
I blush to think that I could ever have been so
hypocritical.　I remember that one Sunday
afternoon at the Grenes', while Mrs. Grene was
carefully explaining to us a text out of Jere-
miah or Deuteronomy (she had a peculiar pre-
dilection for the most dismal parts of the Old
Testament, and once suggested that we should
have a week day class to read Josephus)—I
remember that I was sitting in the window
when suddenly I saw Bran Boullter walking
with Susy Prague, the most giddy-pated little

bud in town, who had been rushed into society by five or six men, and had immediately assaulted every respectable prejudice therein with awful audacity and success. Bitterness of vexation and jealousy suddenly filled my soul. I felt as if I should like to jump out of the window, tear Susy from the side of Mr. Boullter, carry him off triumphantly across the frozen river, eclipse her in her own sphere and dazzle the city for—for how long?

Here I paused. I said to myself—" Ethel, Susan Prague is a comet. Do you wish to be a comet?" And to such a sensible question there was only one answer. It was pleasant enough to read Shakespeare in Lotty's little class, but it would have been ten times more fun to have read some of the delightful French plays that I skimmed with one eye at the library when no one was looking, and a hundred times more fun to have acted something. As it was few of us could make pretensions to reading well. Never shall I forget Mr. Charter moaning out in lugubrious tones

" The big drops *cursed* one another down his innocent nose."

The mistakes, to be sure, were the most amusing part of the whole affair.

One of our men never swore, and he consequently insisted on leaving out every word which in his opinion remotely resembled an objurgation—the consequence of this being that most remarkable gaps were sometimes left in the conversation. Then the marking of the books—of course we always used stage editions —was productive of some very funny blunders, because it was generally done by the girls, instead of by the men. One girl, I remember, struck out all that Sir Andrew in Twelfth Night says about " the Vapians passing the Equinoctial of Queubus," because she was sure that it was improper ; and another hesitated over Jaques' " Ducdame," till she looked lower down and found that 'twas " a Greek invocation to call fools into a circle." The casting, by the way, was always unsatisfactory. If on one night, for instance, Letty Risquict read Viola, the next night some one else had to have

Rosalind; yet Letty was the only girl who read a heroine decently. Then, when Milly Mortmain took Beatrice, it was impossible for Mr. Temple, who always read the lover, to have Benedick, because it was generally rumored that they had once been engaged, before she came out, and that the families had broken it off.

Yes, I was beginning to forget that only a short time before my great and single aim had been to establish myself firmly. I actually found myself out of humor at several parties because I felt continually an imaginary restraint oppressing me. How did my first Assembly go off, indeed? Bran Boullter, bless him, had my name put on the sacred list of subscribers entirely of his own accord and before any one consulted him on the subject. I waited for the second Assembly with Lotty and the other buds and shared with them the fever of excitement that always precedes that important event. We talked it over among ourselves early and late—recounted the experiences of the older

girls, speculated as to the probability of getting
partners !—all the famous traditions were re-
vived for us and all the old stories retold. We
heard of the great year when nearly a hundred
men of the most ideal elegance came on from
the other cities and when for three days there
were partners enough to satisfy even the
wall-flowers; of the famous Assembly when,
because Mrs. Crocus Snowdrop had thirty-two
bouquets and Violet Morninglory only thirty
one, Morris Japonica rushed out into a driving
snow-storm and returned at midnight with two
bouquets, which he presented to Violet, which
proof of devotion it was, according to common
account, that finished her and won him his triumph ; of the sad Assembly, when the news came
of Patty Caique's elopement, and all the men
who were in love with her were so miserable
that they would speak to nobody ;—our interest
deepened and our excitement grew as we listened not only to these tales, but to tales of
awful discoveries and dire accidents, of great
successes and woful failures—tales that grow

into traditions, traditions that ripen into articles of faith.

I remember saying in the heat of discussion
that if I had no engagements at all, I should
be afraid to enter the room; but as, at the
time, I was engaged for the German and two
waltzes, I fancy that I must have been view-
ing the subject from the standpoint of sentiment, rather than of reason. I was especially
fortunate in being so well thought of. My
waltzes were with Bran Boullter and Mr. Charter, and I had to promise the German to Mr.
Hall. Bran asked me for his waltz very early
in the season, before I knew whether I was
going or not, and nearly took my breath away;
and Mr. Hall was quite early too in engaging
me for the German. But I do not wonder
that men often do not ask girls to dance before
the evening of the ball, for every engagement
means a bouquet, and not all the men in society
are able to afford more than one compliment of
that nature at Assembly time, by any means.
We never thought of that when we were buds,

of course, and I remember that most young
girls considered it quite mean for men to go to
the Assemblies on the chance of picking up a
partner. I think myself it is quite as under-
hand for girls to make their families provide
them with flowers, and I have known some
who were loaded with bouquets to confess privately in the dressing-room that their cards
were absolutely empty. But to return. When
I first entered that gorgeous fôyer my heart
gave a bound! I had once or twice peeped
into it when at the opera, and wondered how
such a bare and uninteresting room could ever
afford the gorgeous spectacle to which I looked
forward with such a beating heart—but now
the place seemed to me a Fairyland. While
we were waiting for Mrs. Hathorne in the
dressing-room, I could hardly restrain myself;
and when we came out into the curving corridor full of flowers and plants, behind which
sat merry couples, thronged with gay promen-
aders, altogether mysterious and wonderful—
when we caught our first glimpse of the

crowded ball-room, saw the blue hangings, heard the crash of the band, I was in the seventh heaven of bliss and excitement. But in a very short time my spirits came down to their level again. It was only an ordinary party on a large scale—very much the same men talked to me, very much the same things were said. I did exactly what I had been doing at every party throughout the winter. I was tired of restraining myself. I wanted to "let out and swipe," as the cricketers say; I wanted to cut a dash. Mrs. Hathorne didn't want Lotty to sit on the stairs; of course that meant that I must stay near her all the evening, or ruin my character with her. If I could have gotten off by myself somewhere, where the eyes of all the old ladies were not fixed on me, I could have given myself free play; it was only when we were sitting on the stairs at supper (every body did that, so Mrs. Hathorne didn't mind), that I managed to get into a corner where I had a quiet flirtation. Otherwise, I danced, or rather tried to dance, for the floor

was awfully crowded, and six or seven men
kept appearing and reappearing, and saying
things I could not hear; and I always felt convinced that I must let Mrs. Hathorne see me
pass by at least once every ten minutes,—and
I was demure—heavens! I looked at those
suggestive doors in the corridor, and would
have given my head to have gone with Bran
Boullter into the pitch-black galleries, or
slipped down to the supper-room, where the
men were now smoking, to see what was going
on—or to have done something exciting, no
matter what! I think Bran felt that I had not
fulfilled his expectations, and in truth I was so
impatient that evening with myself and my
surroundings, that I was once or twice quite
cross to him.

Mrs. Hathorne took us away early. I did
not breathe a sigh. I wanted to go.

But I preached patience to myself with much
diligence; and I dare say that my state of mind
at the Assembly was more gloomy than at any
other time during the winter. When Lent sent

us all into comparative quiet I had fewer temptations and more time to reflect. "After all," I said to myself, " suppose I do not go to wildly gay suppers after the opera, or on racketing sleighing parties with a sham matron—suppose I am forced to curb myself in every way, I ought not to complain, and I am positively ungrateful for so doing. Learn, Ethel, to be contented with what you have achieved. *Tout vient à qui sait attendre.*"

With this maxim, and with the little catchword of which Mr. Temple was so fond,— " Patience, gentlemen, and shuffle,"—I comforted myself. I shuffled. I addressed myself once more to the routine of gaining favors, and tried to like what I had as I had not what I liked. And I think my spirits really rose to a considerable extent.

But the occasions when I really felt superior to the world were those hours when into the delighted ears of Lotty and Olive, I poured my confidences, and for them satirized my acquaintances. Not that I was ill-natured ; but my nerves

were so soothed and my temper so improved by
the process that it was a double pleasure to me.
It was so satisfying to be able to mimic the
little foolish ways of the men, to hit off the
affectations of the girls,—and I could do it in
the best-natured way in the world. Often while
some fussy dowager was drawing on my discretion or my patience, have I said to myself,
" You shall pay for this, my dear lady! Shall
I not remember your bonnet strings, and your
ridiculous waist, and that egregious false front?
Be careful about the pronunciation of your
French, I beg, or I shall be tempted at some
future time to imitate you." And oh, the men
who patronized me! It was such fun to see
them bowing to Lotty or Olive on the evenings
of the days on which we had been laughing at
them. It was so delightful to pretend inno-
cence, to lead them on in their folly! I protest,
I believe a girl can make a man say or think
any thing! Well, I may have been ill-natured,
but consider the provocation.

Towards the end of Lent I decided on a little

offensive strategy, and got up a couple of small Saturday afternoon teas. Of course, Lotty and Olive came to my assistance. I decked up our comparatively bare walls with a hundred or so of Japanese fans which I got for a few cents apiece; and, in a moment of inspiration, conceived the happy thought of covering our dresses also with the airy adornments.

I was enormously successful, and the men who straggled in to my first tea were so much amused by the *tout ensemble*, that they beat up all the afternoon loungers, and for the last hour on our first afternoon, and all through the second, the little parlor was perfectly jammed. This success gave me an idea of a new outlet for my energies, and at the end of my first winter I longed more than ever to play a different *rôle* in society. Finally, one day when I was thinking over my prospects for the next season, I hit on the simple solution of all my difficulties —Marriage! I can honestly say that it had never occurred to me before in exactly that light; and when I first thought of it, it gave

me a little chill even while I exulted in the idea
of being my own mistress and a matron in
Israel.   Now I saw why my mother wished me
to be discontented with the present state of
affairs.   Now I saw how I could obtain such a
foothold as would give me the right to defy
criticism.   Yet I gave the subject every consideration.   At one time I nearly put the idea
quite away from me and decided, in accordance
with some romantic notions I had in my head,
to wait until I really fell in love no matter
what might happen in the meantime.   But was
it at all sure that I should fall in love? while I re-
mained in my present state of mind, so I argued, I should all the time be wishing for more
liberty.   "I know men too well, already,"
thought I, "and I have only two more winters in
which to find the man of my heart.   For the matter of that, am I not too calculating in my disposition for it to be probable that I ever shall fall in
love in any desperate fashion?   On the other
hand, what do I gain by deciding to have
all the fun I can before settling down?"   I

counted up the girls I knew who had made
good matches, and I found that most of them
had taken their opportunities at best and gone
off at least early in their second winters; and
this was especially true of girls who, like myself,
had had no money. On the whole I decided
that matrimony was my racket, as Bran Boullter would have expressed it; and having made
up my mind I immediately proceeded to select
a husband. For I had to marry somebody;
and to wait until a *mariage de raison* presented
itself would have been, under the circumstances, quite as foolish as to wait for a *mariage
d'amour.* O men, men!—but, dear me, if I
apostrophize them, and warn them that they
do not know what is going on in the minds of
the demure beings whom they patronize and
protect, they can perfectly well reply that we
do not always comprehend the creatures whom
we consider so coarse and stupid. Alas, I am
afraid the human race is deceitful as a class!

It was only natural that when once I began to
think over my male acquaintance I should first

breathe "with a twin-born sigh" the name of
my adored Bran. I mused over his charms for
a while, but soon put the thought from me and
proceeded to business, for I was not sure that I
cared for him more than most girls did, nor
was I at all sure of my ability to overcome him.
Moreover, he was poor; but I must frankly confess that just as this thought crossed my mind
I caught myself humming "The desert were a
paradise—If thou wert there! If thou wert
there!" Dear Bran! But I proceeded to business, and after disposing of one or two other
men—Macy Temple, for instance, for whom I
felt much friendship but no particular affection,
and who was quite as poor as Mr. Boullter—
I soon decided, with a reservation in favor of
any body more eligible who might turn up in the
meantime, upon Mr. Charter. My reasons were
convincing. Penn Charter was young, healthy to
a degree, very rich, of simply unsurpassable position, and quite good natured. I knew that if I
once succeeded in charming him his natural
obstinacy would make him marry me in spite

of his mother, who was a scraggy, jewely old
lady, of unconscionable pride and dense ig-
norance, with a violent temper and a cock-
ade on her footman's hat. I was not much
scared by the prospect of hostilities with
her, and I knew that if I once got Mr. Charter to fall in love with me I could keep him
fond of me as long as I wished. My mind was
naturally much stronger than his, and if I married him I should have the satisfaction of marrying a man whose habits as well as his birth
were gentlemanly, and who was too little accustomed to slowness in his daily life to object
to a trifle of rapidity in mine. When I had
entirely made up my mind I again took up the
use of my eyes and shot several damaging
glances at him before he left town. In the
meantime I gave my mother an inkling of
what was passing in my mind. I threw out
careless hints and sound generalities on the subject of marrying well and settling down, with
which she was, of course, highly pleased, and
finally, without actually telling her the name of

the man whom I hoped to meet there, I succeeded in getting her to agree that it would be
a good thing for my prospects if we could go
to Narragansett for the month of August.

I could not bring myself to speak openly—it
seemed to me too abominably indelicate to declare my intentions regarding any man, even to
my own mother; and, I am afraid, I thought
as much of a little farewell flirtation with Mr.
Boullter in the first two weeks of the month as
I did of making play on Mr. Charter in the last
two. I knew their movements, of course; that
summer all the young men went to Narragansett.

IV.

AH, how I remember the ecstatic bliss of those delicious afternoons, when I stretched myself out on the brown rocks with Bran by my side, looking out on the bright quickly-moving sea, or along the sun-burned coast to where lay Newport, mystical and suggestive, shimmering in the hazy horizon! In spite of all Bran's attractions I longed at times to sail over to that magic harbor and see for myself if there were really yachts and drags and magnificent heroes and gorgeous times, as there were reported to be. At Narragansett there were two things to do—"rock" in the afternoon with Mr. Boullter, "piazza" in the evening with Bran. The beach, the Studio, the Lighthouse, the hops, were as nothing in comparison. Ah, how I remember how we used to start out in the cool sea-breeze! while we trudged along the dusty road, I

thought only of the envy caused in every
feminine breast by my easy possession of this
tall and graceful creature swinging along beside me, with his bronzed complexion and
golden curls, his beautiful coats and careless
carriage—but when we had passed the black
and dusty pier and had begun to tread the
crisp grasses and huckleberries I saw the sweep
of the horizon before me, and thought only of
Bran and romance!

At last his two weeks were up. I prepared
myself for the parting and made up my mind
to draw the curtain upon the last bit of poetry
in my life—but, to my surprise, he did not go!
At first I was inclined to be a little angry, and
fancied that he would interfere with my designs
on Mr. Charter, but on second thoughts I was
very glad he was still on the ground. For, I
reflected, if I make a dead set at Mr. Charter,
he will dodge me, but, as he has never taken
the trouble to consider that the real private attitude of most girls towards him must be that
of indifference, he will be confused if I can

make him think that I am repelling his advances.
If, then, I first make him believe that he is
cutting out Mr. Boullter and then am cavalier
with him, he will be piqued, and it will be easy
enough for me to lead on. But I must watch·
my chances carefully—in vain is the net spread
in the sight of any bird!

My reasoning was quite just, and the only
flaw in my scheme was that Mr. Boullter might
see through it—but I comforted myself by
thinking that he would not take the trouble to
ponder deeply over the reasons which led me to
smile on Mr. Charter, and that having had two
weeks of me he himself was probably preparing
to worship some other divinity before my very
eyes.

Before going any further I must recount an
affair that made me somewhat dissatisfied with
myself. In making a choice among the young
men of my acquaintance I had thought for a
moment of Mr. Hall, but had decided that his
character was too lofty and severe for me to be
able to make much of an impression on him. I

had come to regard him with a mixture of
awe, liking, and impatience. His conversation
was at times more profoundly interesting to me
than that of any other man I knew; and at
other times he bored me horribly. He was
grave without being at all gloomy, and his
manner and address always excited my greatest
respect and admiration. Possessed of a large
fortune, he had devoted himself to study, and
had already written a law book that had been
highly praised. I knew well that at some
future day he would be a very distinguished
man, and a faint flutter agitated my heart at
the thought of being his wife; but I did not
think myself at all up to his standard, and possibly I may also have shuddered at the prospect
of being too good. At any rate, I never attrib-
uted the decorous attentions he paid me to
any thing but his feelings concerning my father,
about whom he spoke to me several times, and
though I frequently got into very earnest discussions with him, and on more than one
occasion hopelessly lost myself in the endeavor

to comprehend his explanations of modern theories and the philosophy of history and such deep subjects (I remember that he talked to me one whole evening about Hypatia, which I had just been reading, and though I was desperately interested, I scarcely understood half of what he said, and only got a general impression that people had begun to be wicked as soon as they became Christians and had not grown better as time wore on)—still, I accounted for his attentions on the score of his general fondness for discussion and his willingness to instruct ignorant little geese like myself.

And I suppose I had an innate dislike for his consistency. He was curiously punctilious, and almost irrational in his regard for singleness of conduct. He never spoke of his ideas in any way as if he was thinking of himself as the example of his own gospel—he would as soon have discussed with you his razors or his wristbands—but he often told me that he admired nothing so much as absolute constancy to one's word in every thing; and he never

5

would let any consideration affect or change his mind. This I could not understand—it was utterly foreign to my nature. I learned from him to be silent when things did not go as I wished them to go, but his calmness was almost the repose of the elements, and my apparent meekness was compounded of the simples of mellow hypocrisy and suppressed ill-temper. Otherwise Mr. Hall was often a vexation to my spirit. Some people called him a prig, but he was not. His finer feelings were—but all his feelings were fine! They used to say that once when he was walking through the country, he met a poor woman who was an epileptic. Just after he had passed her she fell into a fit. He turned to help her; and the story was that he was discovered sitting by the side of a brook to which he had carried the woman, waiting for her to recover and gravely sailing his hat in the water to amuse her little boy. This sounds somewhat like Kenelm Chillingly, but he did not in the least resemble that half legendary hero.

Although my wits had been sharpened by reason of my greater familiarity with the subject, I never suspected him of being in love with me, and he certainly never showed his affections in the way that other young men do.

One evening we had arranged some tableaux at the hotel, and it was decided to finish the entertainment with that clever little sketch, *Place aux Dames.* I was Lady Macbeth. Now Lady Macbeth has to say, somewhere or other, (I forget exactly how it goes), that Ophelia, who is always quoting what " Ham says," talks as if she were a sandwich, for she never says two words without putting a slice of *Ham* in between. When I opened my mouth for this biting sarcasm on poor Ophelia (who was played by oh, such a lovely Baltimore girl!) I looked over towards the windows of the dining-room in which the stage had been set up, and at one of them, just down by the foot of the stage, gracefully resting his elbows on the ledge and leaning in, was Mr. Boullter. Mechanically, I went on with my speech, but was suddenly

aroused by a horribly amused smile on his face
to the consciousness that I had declared that
Ophelia (who was giggling at the side scenes)
couldn't say two words without putting a slice
of *Bran* in between! For a moment I was
covered with confusion, but recovered myself
and went on stoutly, puffing myself out to look
more Lady Macbeth-ian than ever. I don't
think any body but Ophelia and Bran himself
noticed my little slip; certainly Juliet didn't,
for she asked me afterwards what made me
blush so violently. After the play was over
Bran came up to me and said that I had been
" murdering *his* sleep," for the last two weeks,
and that he proposed to do execution on a
little of mine in return. " You mustn't go to
bed yet," he said. " Come and take a turn or
two on the porch before you turn in." It was
a night for romance if ever there was one. The
moon hung high in the dusky heavens, and
any body who has ever been to Rhode Island
knows how black and smooth its swelling tide
can be, how bright and mysterious are the re-

flections of its lights dancing on the water, how warm and full of whisperings is its gentle breeze. It was but a step from the hotel to the beach—but that step cost! As we sat together in front of the row of bathing-houses, Bran's voice became more and more intoxicating, his face drew nearer and nearer to mine, and I closed my eyes and said to myself, "If he chooses to kiss me—why he may—that's all!" And of course he did.

I am simply stating the facts as they occurred and I am not attempting to excuse myself; but if all the girls whom Bran Boullter has kissed were to own up, it is my private opinion that the list would be enormous.

As I opened my eyes, and while we were still, to say the least, in a very unconventional position, a figure in bathing costume came slowly out of the little alley just beside us, halted for a brief instant in surprise at seeing us there, and then hastened down to the water's edge and sprang into the breakers. I pressed Bran's hand, which was somehow or other clasping mine, violently in my emotion, and then tore my own away, gasping out, " Goodness! he must have seen us!" Bran took things rather calmly, and, in fact, began to laugh in what I considered a very callous manner. But he only laughed for an instant and then said:

"It's only Middleton Hall. I entirely forgot that that queer lad indulges his natatory predilections whenever there is moonlight. Bless you, he never saw you, being at present meditating philosophy, which does not make him uncommon lively in his perceptions, and if he did see you," he continued, in a more serious tone, " he could not by any possibility have recognized you."

I was calmed after a little while by Bran's assurances, and by the fact that it really was quite dark under the roof of the bathing houses, but my moral nerves had received too great a shock to permit of my continuing the flirtation, so we returned to the hotel, which Bran said he was loath to do.

Shall I ever forgive myself for my folly? The next day we went on a drive to the Light House. Mr. Hall joined me as, after leaving the carriage, we were walking towards the rocks. Somehow or other something was said about swimming, and I promptly remarked that I had seen him taking one of his nocturnal swims! I could have bitten my tongue off! He turned and looked at me quickly in a curious manner; and all at once I began to feel my old fear of him entirely possessing me. I blushed. I simply stood still and blushed; and as I felt the hot color burning my cheeks, I could see the look in his face turn into one of pain and astonishment,—and then his forehead contracted into a frown and he half turned away. By this time I was in a state of dreadful nervousness, and, scarcely knowing what I did, I stammered out:

"Oh, Mr. Hall! please don't think—please don't say—"

He turned to me again, and began to speak in a low dignified tone.

"I beg," he said, "that you will overlook my great want of self-command. If you will allow me to speak for a moment of matters upon which I really have no right to touch, you will perhaps pardon my lack of discretion. I must begin," said he, frowning a little again, "by telling you what I have at times hoped you had discovered; that my attentions to you arose from a serious admiration of your generous disposition, your great refinement," (this was the result of my demureness!) "and the attractive qualities of your mind. But this interest in you, while it may explain the impulse which led me to discover what otherwise I would not have allowed myself to suspect, and though it will never cease to cause me to desire your happiness, must now cease to prompt me to hope for my own; for it would be idle in me to pretend that what I have unintentionally found out is not perfectly clear to me. And though I have no right to comment upon it, I I can at no other time better ask you to forgive me for being so injudicious. Allow me to express to you, my dear Miss Jones, my greatest respect and give you my best wishes; and though I cannot help framing a suspicion as to the identity of the happy man, I promise you that I will not even think of congratulating him until your engagement is actually announced. Forgive me, once more for my lack of self-control, and pray do not judge it too hardly."

This was too much. My feelings during this polite but really heart-rending speech were so conflicting that, when he stopped and looked at me gravely and sadly, I could hardly help screaming with laughter. But I was still awfully afraid of him, and I could only stammer out the truth.

" Oh, dear me, Mr. Hall! " I said, " Oh, I don't know what you'll think—but I—I'm not engaged to Mr. ——, I'm not engaged to any body —and," I added desperately, " I'm not going to be ! "

For a moment or two he did not speak, and the expression of his face hardly changed,

but he gave a slight start when I first spoke.
Then he said, in his deepest tones :

"Then I am happy that you are still in such
a position that I may offer you my hand and
heart, sincerely ——" Here he broke off for a
minute and then went on to say something
about that being hardly the place in which he
had looked forward to asking me to be his wife
—but I could not listen to him. Heavens!
What a fool I felt myself to be! And how
noble he was! And yet, despite my admiration for him, I was very much vexed with him.
I could not understand it! Why, why, when
he found that the girl he liked had been flirting outrageously with another man did he not
give his bridle rein a shake and say adieu for-
evermore? This was his abominable punctil-
iousness! This was his consistency! How
beautifully he had entangled himself, first by
his insane habit of explaining himself, and then
by his more insane habit of refusing to take the
fair advantage of the game! It is true that he
may not have seen any thing particular—he may

only have inferred from my blushing that something had happened—I protest I don't know to this day exactly what he thought, and I cannot decide with any satisfaction to myself. But I remember what my own thoughts were like! I could hear the chattering of some people behind us, and their inane laughter clattering about the rocks. I longed to sit down just where I was and cry! But I shook myself together. Come, Ethel Jones! said I—have you no force of character at all? At first I felt as if I had swallowed the mucilage bottle, but I motioned to Mr. Hall, who was still speaking slowly and gravely (Heaven knows what he was saying!) and began bravely enough.

"Oh, Mr. Hall," I said, "if admiration and respect could make me want to marry you, it would be easy to say yes. But you must not think of me any more. I cannot marry you—you would not be happy if I did."

Here I paused—for want of matter. Mr. Hall was listening gravely; he made a slight gesture of protest. I tried for speech once more—I had no idea of what I was going to say. But I restrained Mr. Hall by convulsive waves of my hand and presently got my voice, only to lose it again. I gasped out a few words—bade him to forget me—said that I didn't know what he would think of me, and desired him not to say any thing more to me about it—" for," said I, with a great gulp, " my nerves won't stand it ! " And I walked up to the Light House as fast as possible.

Thus did Ethel Jones, the clever, the self-composed, the perspicacious Ethel Jones fail utterly in her first crisis ! I can fairly say that with any other man it would have been different ; but Mr. Hall magnetized me and, by the superior weight of his character, compelled me to exhibit myself in my baldest colors. During the rest of the afternoon I kept laughing feebly to myself while thinking of the picture that I should have presented if I had given way at the critical moment—seated in a stagnant rock-pool at the feet of Middleton Hall and weeping

bitterly! I was terribly disgusted with myself;
I longed to be able to go through it all over
again so that I might try to come off successful, yet at the same time I could not help feeling that I had done something vaguely heroic in
throwing away such a chance. In fact I do not
know which was the stronger feeling—my vain
regret or my unwarrantable pride. After thinking it over for some days I came to the conclusion that after having betrayed myself by that
wretched blush I had done the best thing possible in refusing him instead of trying to keep
my hold on him, for I felt confident that if he
had ultimately married me it would have been
only from his sense of honor, and he would
have been miserably unhappy to think he was
marrying a flirt. And now, I said to myself, it's
all over, once for all, and I can begin my pursuit
of Penn Charter without being distracted by
thoughts of any other man. But though I
agreed with myself I was not by any means
satisfied. When I returned to town I got
together a copy of Matthew Arnold and a

beautiful little set of Macaulay's works that Mr. Hall had given to me and sent them to his club with a note saying that in view of what had occurred I did not feel justified in keeping them. I received a brief answer thanking me for my note and telling me that he was going to Heidelberg for the winter to study Roman Law. So, with a sigh in which disappointment and virtue still struggled for the mastery I bade him adieu—and he rode away.

But to return to Narragansett and Mr. Charter. When I came to begin my campaign in earnest I found that I was by no means as confident as I had been. Perhaps the adventure of which I have just been speaking made me doubt the soundness of my foresight and judgment. I certainly felt nervous and perhaps depressed; and I was a little at a loss how to proceed. Luckily Mr. Charter did not come to Narragansett for several days after Mr. Hall had gone away, so my general tone had a chance to improve. Moreover, I was favored by chance while I was still debating as to whether my

plan of operations really deserved the name of
good generalship—and I was not so undecided
that I could not instantly take advantage of my
opportunities.

It was on the day after Mr. Charter's arrival
that several of us had been chatting together on
the beach after bathing—digging our feet into
the sand, idly flinging little stones into the
water, commenting sarcastically upon the rest
of our acquaintance—and one by one the others
had dropped off until Daisy Canayle and I were
left alone with Mr. Boullter and Mr. Charter.
Daisy Canayle was a rather horrid girl from
somewhere in the interior of New York. The
Canayles were absolutely nobody, and no one
ever heard of them in the winter; but Daisy
always came out at watering-places, to which I
fancy her family took her for matrimonial reasons. Just now she was divided in her mind as
to which of the men she wanted to insnare.
On the one hand there was the temptation to
take Bran away from me; yet, I am quite sure
she thought that she might get more out of

Penny, for she was an awfully mercenary little
wretch, and was always ogling men who were
known to send bouquets or who had dog-carts—
besides which she used to cast her bread upon
the waters by giving presents so that return
might be made in kind. When I found myself
alone in her company I determined to depart ;
but I checked myself almost immediately and
said, "Wait, Ethel, till you see what is going to
happen."

As I expected she finally made up her mind
that Penny was her better game. She was
lying on the sand leaning her cheek on her
hand. Her hair—she really had magnificent
hair—was pretending to be drying, and she had
it gathered away from the sand and flung over
her shoulder. Artless thing! I knew what was
coming.

"Oh, dear me," she said, with a glance out of
her eyes at Mr. Charter—"Oh dear me! This
sea-bathing is horribly bad for my hair—it is
splitting at the end, every bit of it !"

"What a pity," said Bran, laughing.

"Oh go on, my dear!" said I to myself. "You think Penny Charter an innocent because his remarks are not those of a Talleyrand or a Sheridan. I could tell you better than that."

"Look, Mr. Charter!" cried she, guilelessly, taking up a wisp of the article under discussion—"just look and see if it isn't."

He took it and smoothed it between his fingers, blushing a little, saying something moderately polite. This was my opportunity. Just as he was withdrawing his hand I sat a little further away from them and smiled a faint, pitying smile at Bran. Penny saw me, as I intended he should. Of course if the little flirtation had been of his own seeking he would only have been stimulated by my smile into further advances; but as it was he could hardly help feeling that it had been thrust upon him, and consequently he at once desired to be of my party. I saw him pause a little, and I knew my point was gained. Accordingly, while Daisy—who had not seen the by-play—went on making more and more of a set at him, drib-

6

bling sand through her rosy little fingers and tossing audacious grains of it towards him, humming little bits of the songs of the season, showing more and more of her delicate ankles —(dark blue stockings with white polka dots and Oxford ties look very well under a pink lawn skirt)—all this while, I say, I leaned back calmly and talked in a dignified manner to Bran, favoring Penny with one or two more smiles judiciously timed. Presently another man, one of the enthusiastic bathers who was only just through his morning swim, came up, and I rose feeling that I would not have to leave Bran alone with Daisy—as I might have had to do, though it would have been rather hard on him. Penny jumped up at the same time.

" I say," he said to me rather eagerly, "won't you come and have some clams at the Studio?"

" Yes—certainly," said I ; and I moved a step or two to show him I was quite ready.

" Let us go, then," said he, and off we went, leaving Daisy still sitting on the sand with

rather a blank expression on her lovely
face.

I threw a bewitching glance over my shoulder
at the three behind me. "Yes, love," said I,
under my breath, "you may walk all the way
up to the hotel with your hair over your shoulders, and much good may it do you!"

If I ever delighted the soul of a man I delighted the soul of Penn Charter that day. We
got a seat next to the window and looked out
on the yellow sands and the tumbling waves
and the extraordinary old women who always
bathe at times when they are the only persons
to be seen—a sort of proclamation, I suppose,
that they know they are so ugly that it is use-
less for them to try to conceal it. I was in a
humor to be charming—and charming I was.
Touch *my* hair, indeed? Before our little lunch
was over he thought it the highest favor to
have been allowed to tell me that I was losing
a hair-pin—and I blushed as he told me. As
he left me at the hotel he asked me to go
driving with him that afternoon, and I con-

sented with a half-smile, a half-blush, and a half-courtesy—and I felt that I was now fairly started.

But I had a good deal of trouble. Daisy Canayle was simply furious, and made up her mind at once to cut me out if possible ; and as she didn't care what she did when she had once determined on any thing, she came very near inveigling Penny into a desperate flirtation with her. Luckily, she had been a good deal talked about that summer, and the gossips had kindly prepared a reputation for her, so that she did not possess the spice of mystery. If she had, I am afraid she would have been successful, for she was, oh, wonderfully pretty! and a man might well have felt that he would have given

> *"* "All other bliss,
> And all his worldly worth for this,
> To waste his whole heart in one kiss
> Upon her perfect lips "

if he had been quite sure that some other man had not done it before him. So that all I had to do was to be dignified and charming; for it would have been fatal to allow Penny once to suspect that I was competing with Daisy.

I took good care not to let myself pass out of his mind in the empty autumn months. I arranged matters so that he forgot some important matter that I had promised to talk over with him until just as I boarded the train for home, and after I had led him on to begging to be allowed to write to me about it I gave a half-doubting consent and made the boon so much more precious in his eyes. When he came back to town, therefore, my nets were still tight about him. I had really grown quite fond of him by that time; and when he began once more to be attentive to me I found myself blushing secretly about it, feeling foolishly uneasy when he did not appear, and just as foolishly pleased when he did. But I did not let the world perceive it, as may well be imagined, and as Mr. Boullter still kept hovering round me, I was rather glad to have him as a foil. Finally, one afternoon in January, matters came to the conclusion for which I had at first hoped and of which I now dreamed.

Mr. Charter had asked me to go sleighing with him. Frosty was the air and blue the sky, and· as we skimmed along the road above the frozen pools of the Wissahickon, the sleigh-bells tinkling merrily under the rising lifts of pine and spruce, I am afraid that I leaned a little against the warm top-coat of my swain, and probably incited him to the taking of the step which I did not anticipate just then. He turned the horse suddenly as we came to a road that wandered down from somewhere on top of the hill above us, and soon, when we stopped, after ascending the hill, I looked delightedly over the rolling country about us and breathed deeper the sharp air that set my cheeks aglow and through whose clear expanse we saw the distant villages and farm houses distinct against the pale horizon. We had not spoken for some little time; Penny touched the horse and we entered the woods again. Then he drew off his big otter-skin glove—I had been wanting to stroke it all the afternoon—and laid his hand on mine, which happened just then to be lying on the robe.

"Ethel," said he. "I want you to—I—that is—look here, Ethel, I—I love you!"

I was rather surprised, so I drew back a little —but in a moment I realized the situation and thrilled and blushed with pleasure. I have already said that I grew much prettier in my second winter, and dare say that just then I was a very pleasurable sight ; at any rate poor Penny appeared to think so, for he dropped the reins and extended both hands to me, calling out :

"Oh do say yes! do say yes! I shall be broken-hearted if you don't!"

I breathed rather quickly and then leaned towards him with a smile, which I suppose he considered to be quite a sufficient answer, for in a moment his arms were about me. Why are men's arms so awfully big when they have on their overcoats and gloves? I felt as if I were in the embrace of an affectionate bear, and I gave a hysterical little giggle as the thought occurred to me, and then I felt perfectly happy.

But there remains something else to be told before I begin to recount the experiences of my married life.

The next evening I was seated all alone in our little parlor contemplating a basket of lovely roses which Penny had sent me. I was alone, because I had insisted that he should go to a dinner at Mrs. Feedham's, though he wanted to stay away ; and I was now enjoying myself by fancying the manner in which the news of our engagement would be received—I had resolved to announce it on the night of the second Assembly, of course. I had insnared my *promesso sposo* very quietly. Several girls had congratulated me on my supposed engagement to Mr. Boullter, but nobody had suspected the true state of affairs. So much wrapped up was I in my contemplation that I must have entirely forgotten to say that I was not at home, and if I did hear the door bell ring it could have made no impression on me, for I suddenly looked up to see Bran himself closing the parlor door behind him. I rose somewhat abruptly, and began to consider whether I could ask him to excuse me. My eye was caught by something unusual in his appearance, and I looked at him attentively. He was not in evening dress, a thing remarkable in itself, and his hair was a little more tumbled than usual; but I chiefly noticed a sort of determined look about his face. He came quickly forward and took my hand, which he pressed eagerly.

"My dear little girl!" he said—my heart gave a leap and then—sank. I knew what was going to happen. "My dear little girl!" he repeated, "I say that to you, Ethel, because I'm in love with you." Then he paused for a moment and went on: "I won't say it again if you object, you know."

"Mr. Boullter," said I, as calmly as possible, "I'm very sorry to hear you say so, and I think I had better tell you that I am engaged."

"Oh heavens!" he said, starting and looking

awfully taken aback, " you don't say that—you don't mean to say you're engaged to somebody else, do you?"

"I am engaged to Mr. Charter," said I.

"Now don't get up," he said quickly. "Let me speak to you for a minute, you know. I dare say I oughtn't to ask you to do it, but you needn't fear personal violence; I sha'n't break the furniture—or do any high tragedy."

I made up my mind to listen, and he went on, looking away from me and clenching his hands together.

"You see," he said, "I expected that you would say that I wasn't good enough, or that I was too confounded lazy, or that you would prefer a more first-class article—and I thought that I might argue the point with you and get you to give me a chance—but to find you engaged to another man is bewildering. I didn't want to fall in love, you see, and I had been laying myself out to cure myself all winter; but last night I saw you, and by Jove! I couldn't stand it. And to-day I argued it all over with myself; and I stayed away from Mrs. Feedham's dinner because I heard you weren't going, and came to see you. Well," said he, with a big sigh, " Penny Charter is a good fellow—and a devilish lucky man! Don't be too sorry for me; I dare say that my trivial nature will soon recover; and it may please you to hear that you're the only girl I ever proposed to—I'll take an affidavit to it, if you like. I have succumbed at last. My scalp is gone and my glory has departed. Good-by!"

I think there was a tear in my own eye as I shook hands with him, and I know that his glistened. As the front door shut behind him, I never felt more like crying in my life. Not that I had discovered too late that I was in love with him ; but I was so awfully sorry for him. I never imagined that I was going to make him fall in love with me; I thought he was girl-proof. I wouldn't have done it for worlds, I said to myself, mournfully. If it had been Neddy Tryffleham, indeed, I should have considered myself a public benefactor! but

dear Bran! So I mused, and so I mourned
over him. I didn't mind his thinking me a
flirt one bit, because he had always been a most
egregious flirt himself. I regarded it as the
irony of fate, and wished that it could have
been proper for me to have patted his head
and told him how sorry I was. I had just arrived at this point in my reflections when the
parlor door once more opened (how on earth
could I have expected *two* people on one
night?) and in walked—Middleton Hall!
"Good gracious," I said to myself, "*he* has
come to propose to me too!" This was too
much. He walked towards me, looking rather
pale, but very dignified and lofty. He was in
full evening dress, and I could not help wondering whether he had brought home a new
crush hat from Lincoln and Bennett's.

"This is an unexpected pleasure, Mr. Hall,"
I said, wishing inwardly it were all over.

"I arrived here only this morning, Miss
Jones," said he. "I have come direct from
Havre. I will tell you, without further preface,

that I have come home on your account. It has seemed to me that your conduct last summer was an evidence of great sincerity and a generous character, and I have been unable to forget you. I wish to tell you that I still love you, and to ask you to be my wife."

"Oh, Mr. Hall!" I stammered, "this time I *am* engaged."

He walked over to the fireplace and stood looking into it for a few minutes, while I felt horribly nervous. Then he came back to where I was sitting.

"I ought not to have gone abroad," he said. "I ought not to have doubted you at all. It is my own fault. I think I have heard you sing the little Heidelberg song—have I not? '*Ach, Scheiden und Meiden thut Weh!*' I find it true. Good-by."

There was a solemnity about the awfulness of this last occurrence which I did not by any means appreciate at the time. I knew it was awful; but I was so very much pleased with Penny and myself, that I really did not give the matter a second thought. I dismissed it from my mind and returned to my engagement. And I am glad I did so, for it saved me from unpleasant reflections. I was married in April, at St. Mark's, of course. I had six brides-maids, Lotty being the first. Bran made it quite evident that he would like to have an ushership, and he was accordingly given one, and every thing was most successful. My presents were gorgeous, and Mrs. Charter, who had threatened not to go to the church, came round some time before the ceremony and behaved in a really noble manner. As Lotty put me into the carriage she whispered to me her engagement to Macy Temple, and I left my mother the happiest woman in Philadelphia.

V.

WE went to Europe on our bridal tour and were there three months.

As neither of us cared much for the *dolce far niente* of Venice we spent most of our time in London and Paris, which two cities Penny knew thoroughly. He took me to quite a number of extraordinary little places which are rarely known by Americans. I am afraid that at any rate he preferred Lord's Ground to South Kensington and St. Stephen's to the Albert Hall. I insisted on my privilege as a married woman and accompanied him to St. Stephen's Hall and to the cafés chantants in Paris. I am bound to say they were remarkably amusing, and they certainly delighted Mr. Charter. He used to go about Paris humming, " *Voyez-vous ce b'garçon là*," just like any gamin. There were one or two other places in Paris to

which I must confess I had a great desire to go.
Penny went off by himself to see some trained
animals at the Folies Bergères, which he said
were very good; but he absolutely refused to
go again and take me, which I considered very
mean in him, especially as I had made no objection to his going alone; and after that I
didn't dare mention Mabille. I don't know
how I brought myself to leave the Parisian
theaters—but I was really growing a little
weary of *tête-à-tête* fun, and my new habili-
ments cried to me with many rustlings not to
let their seams get rubbed nor their foldings
permanent. Penny had behaved like an angel
as to Worth, and though I three times left him
at the hotel laboring under the impression that
I was going to the galleries instead of to the
magasins of the Louvre, he never so much as
winked at the bills nor lamented that he had
not been by my side to check me. It was a
new and delicate pleasure to be shopping for
male approbation. Penny and I had some very
amusing times over my purchases; he really

came to view lace insertions from an artistic
standpoint. I succeeded in persuading a perfect little treasure of a Frenchwoman whom I
met at the Bon Marché to return with me as
my maid; and my bonnets and gowns were absolute triumphs. (Any body can buy a Derby
hat, an ulster, and dogskin gloves or masculine
looking umbrellas, though I have known girls
to come back from England actually pink with
pride in their own cleverness in being able to
purchase just such articles of raiment—but it
isn't every body who can get her own bonnets.
This I say for the benefit of my masculine
readers—and by getting bonnets I don't mean
putting yourself, body and soul into the
hands of a clever Frenchwoman, by any means).
But, though it seemed as if we had been buying a
a great deal, we only had to get five extra trunks.

Any body who has ever voyaged home from
a foreign land will know how delighted I was
when I awoke to find that the miserable screw
had stopped and that out of our porthole I
could see, dim and misty in the early morning,

the outline of Sandy Hook. We went directly
to Newport, where we had been fortunate
enough to get a cottage for the last half of the
season; and that very afternoon I found myself on the big Sound steamer, the Bristol, smiling at the difference between her deck and that
of the Britannic, and between the East River
and the waste of waters to which I had grown
accustomed. While I was thus employed, and
as if to give me a foretaste of the pleasures in
store for me, Penny, who had left me for a moment, came back with a couple of men at his
side, and at the sight of the tallest of them I
smiled to myself a smile of contentment, for I
felt that the pleasures of my married life had
now begun. This man—the tallest—was Kaaterskill Langton, and the other, whom I did not
know, was presented to me as Captain Brague.
They obtained a couple of the ridiculous little
camp-stools that stand about on the decks of
the Sound steamers, and sat down beside me.
Now that I could do so I took a good look at
Mr. Langton. He was a tall, rather heavy man

of extremely English and elegant appearance, and his clothes had that absolutely simple and correct air that proclaims the genius of swellness. He looked worn, but his expression was kindly, and he turned in his toes as he tipped back his chair in a manner that instantly proclaimed high birth and a genteel education. Captain Brague was a jolly looking man with a beautiful figure. He was dressed quite as well as Mr. Langton himself and he wore a *garotte* collar with more easy grace than I had ever seen shown by any man before.

"Just come home, have you, Mrs. Charter?" said Mr. Langton. "Oh! And didn't you think Nelly Farren very fetching?"

"Awfully fetching," said I with a smile.

"And isn't Arthur Roberts a card?"

I really felt that I ought not to admit that I knew who Arthur Roberts was, but Mr. Langton's question was put so naturally that I was just going to answer, in spite of Penny's mean amusement at my hesitation, when Captain Brague interrupted me.

"There you are again," said he, "with your precious topical songs. What on earth does Mrs. Charter care for a beastly comic singer of the present day? If you're in for song, tip us some Lever now——"

It was then that I perceived that the Captain was an Irishman.

"A gentleman of Tom Moore's time," he continued, "would be singing 'Love's Young Dream,' or 'The Young May Moon' to Mrs. Charter; but I'll be bound if you were to serenade her you'd begin with 'The Two Obadiahs!'"

Mr. Langton smiled amiably. "Wait till we get to Newport before you begin your serenading, won't you?" said he to his friend. "I assure you," he continued, turning to me, "he's a regular Blondel."

"Where *is* your cottage?" asked Captain Brague. I had to confess that I did not know the town at all; whereat both of my hearers expressed much surprise. Mr. Langton immediately began to give me an eloquent description of the pleasures and beauties in store for me. "It's a jolly place," he said, "and a beautiful place too. Ask Captain Brague; he's sentimental and he goes in for natural beauty and all that. And you'll have a jolly good time there."

I was not ready to believe just then that any thing could be more engaging than the scenery about me. The sun was beginning to burn deep red in the haze of the lower sky; the breeze on the water was fresh and invigorating, yet warm and full of life—every thing about us was bustle and animation. We were now passing through narrow channels, on the one side of which were high banks on whose crests appeared the streets of the city, sometimes neat and trim, sometimes straggling and decidedly Hibernian, on whose slopes, often rocky and covered with spruce, were crowded a hundred gay arbors and pavilions, from which children in white dresses and smart sashes waved their handkerchiefs at us, and strains of popular music came suddenly to our ears—and on the other side were lower shores, islands with green, well kept lawns and strong, unmistakable, yet picturesque buildings, gravelly beaches, snug little country places with elaborate fences and queer little boat houses standing over the water, into which swept and swung the waves from our great wheel. Later on, when the talkative passengers were subdued and the prudent discarded their dusters for their overcoats; when the schooners which we met were further and further apart; when the waters broadened out and the roar of the city was far behind us; when the sky beyond the low shores on our right hand took on a tinge of dusky blue which suddenly grew pink and then faded out again into distant darkness; when the breeze blew still more soft and pleasant and a lighthouse far ahead showed a twinkling spark just as the first star appeared above us, I felt a great peace of spirit and a happiness. If the way to Newport lies through such scenes as these, I thought, what must Newport be! And when, indeed, I found myself in that earthly paradise, I rejoiced, for my dream of happiness was realized. And what a

change had been made in me in one year's
time.   What a contrast there was between Ethel
Jones and Ethel Charter.   A year ago I had
been an ignorant, though ambitious girl; for
me a dusty row of hotels, a narrow programme
of provincial gayeties, and a foolish romance over
which I could now smile with perfect equanimity had been food for my soul; now I was a
woman, calm and secure; before me was spread
a magnificent landscape, a glittering society;
the life which I was to live was full and stimu-
lating.   "Heavens," I thought to myself, "it is
but a year since Bran Boullter was the sun of
my system—and now I find that he is only a
star in a system so vast that I need a telescope
to see out of it."   I leaned back comfortably
in my coupè and drew my light wrap about
my shoulders, as I drove home from the first
dinner given in my honor—a year before I
would have scampered back to the hotel along
the moonlit shore with Bran by my side.   "I
have much to learn," I thought, "but I can
learn in a day what other women would take

years to comprehend. Let me shake off the last vestiges of my bread-and-butter days and be a woman of the world." If I had pursued such a train of reflections much further I should probably have made an attempt to establish myself as one of the leaders of the mode—as an arbitress in society. But I was still too intent on gayety and enjoyment to care to direct matters which did not amuse me; and I confined myself to the endeavor to be amused in my own way. Mrs. Hannibal St. Joseph, the wife of the great New York capitalist, who, at the time of my arrival,—I cannot say *led*—who *levered* Newport society just as she had been doing for some years, seemed at first to think of trying to crush me by a sort of ponderous imitation of one of her husband's "operations;" but she became very good humored, as soon as she discovered that Penny's fortune had been absurdly over-estimated, and that I was not going to seduce her *chef* from her, nor run rival balls and buy up all the provisions in town, nor make a "corner" in girls or flowers, nor do any thing of that sort; and I thought her first alarm quite as reasonable as her subsequent good nature. Over her I did not care to triumph—but I could not put up with the calm "cheek" of Mrs. Jonas Moderninstance *neè* Esther Mayflower. That cultured Bostonian, (an exceedingly clever woman, I do not deny,) actually thought that I was, or ought to be, afraid of her. I remember that one evening after a dinner at Mrs. St. Joseph's she and I and Kaaterskill Langton had in some manner been thrown together—and she was in a very bad humor. She need not have minded Mr. Langton, who was the best natured man in the world (and every body knows who the Hudson Langtons are)—and as for me, I was at least intelligent. But at dinner she had not been put any where near Professor Dreiddop, the great German Idealist, and he had departed immediately after the repast; and thus she had been unable to put to him her famous question which was understood to have formed the basis of an article by her in the Atlantic Monthly—

as to whether Schopenhauer's pessimism, when read by the light of a sentence from one of Mr. Emerson's Essays, did not appear to be optimism in disguise. While she was sitting with us and still in the sulks on account of her disappointment we somehow began talking of a beautiful Boston girl who moved about in the whirl of society at Newport, calm, pale, lovely and dignified, who smiled like a saint and was supposed to be a sort of mystical compound of medievalism, transcendentalism and erudition— and I very naturally acquiesced in Mrs. Moderninstance's praises of this remarkable young lady; and Mr. Langton said—

"Awf'ly handsome; awf'ly clever, by George, but I can't make her out. Now, a fellow can make out Mrs. Charter, you know—she don't confuse our heads, you know, though she does confuse our hearts. Eh, Mrs. Charter?"

Mrs. Moderninstance went on, still speaking of her young woman:

"I think she may fairly be said to be a type, somewhat sublimated, perhaps, but still dis-

tinctly a type of Northern growth. She is the
result of causes which exist in greater purity
with us in New England than elsewhere ; and
though the exquisite delicacy of such a nervous
system may not be envied by people who have
what are called strong constitutions, I have
often noticed that she excites a feeling of awe
among other girls. Of course our own girls are
accustomed to the type."

" Mr. Langton," said I, " do you know Miss
Cherry Mayson ? "

"Yes, indeed," said he, "an awf'ly jolly girl,
and with lots of pluck—awf'ly plucky, by
Jove ! "

" Do you think," said I, " that she would be
likely to stand in awe of the young lady of
whom Mrs. Moderninstance has been speaking ? "

" Well, I say," answered Mr. Langton, " a
girl who can hold on to the ribbons for nearly
two miles, drive a wicked pony into a hay-cock
and then drop her little brother out behind is
not likely to be afraid of any fellow, you know."

I had calculated that Mr. Langton's answers would be satisfactory.

I knew of what Mrs. Moderninstance had been thinking. A day or two before the said Cherry Mayson, a sufficiently giddy little Philadelphian, had lapsed into complete silence on a sailing party when Mrs. Moderninstance's young woman began to quote Montaigne, and had not spoken again until the company came back to ordinary topics of conversation. I felt very much like repeating to Mrs. Moderninstance Miss Mayson's private comments on the entertainment, but as I happened to know that Mr. Langton had witnessed. Cherry's little adventure I preferred to play that off against the sailing party. But to imagine that a Philadelphia girl of my position would feel awed by any body! I was only impatient with the people who tried to snub me. Being "out for amusement" I did not want to have any trouble in asserting myself—in fact I did not care to be bothered in any way. If, said I to myself, we are epicureans, do let us be

good humored. I found plenty of good humor, begone-dull-care good humor, in the
Langton set, into which Penny and I presently
entered. Katty Langton took quite a fancy to
Penny, and Penny reciprocated his feelings.
We became yachts-people, polo-people ; we had
little suppers *chez vous* and little dinners *chez
nous*. We drove about madly and never conversed very rationally. Most of us could have
conversed rationally, I suppose, but we did not
care to. I may say, in parenthesis, that I did
not take much to the polo. It was a pretty
sight but I soon began to think it very slow
when only two men played on a side. Captain
Brague himself, whom Mr. Langton had brought
over almost expressly for the game, confided to
me that he thought it a beastly pretense at playing, and Penny was somewhat superior, and
could not be persuaded to try it. Still every
body went to the grounds, and it was quite satisfactory to sit on a drag and feel that you were
in it.

The yachting was the supreme pleasure. I

remember one day which Mr. Langton set apart
for some special celebration. He and Penny
had had a grand "spree" the night before—in
fact all our men had taken part in it—and,
though it was whispered that Captain Brague
had "stuck" an unhappy young New Yorker
very badly at piquet, I discovered that Penny
had manfully held his ground. "I don't easily
get taken into camp, you know," said he when
I joked with him about it. But on the morning
of our excursion none of the men looked one
whit the worse for their revelry, and as we cut
through the rippling blue waters between the
Dumplings and the Fort we presented an un-
questionably delightful appearance. We passed
the little Narragansett boat on our way out of
the harbor; and every one on board of her ran
to the side, for the long black lines and tapering
masts of the *Hildegarde* were famous every
where. Katty Langton himself, in full yachting trim, leaned over the taffrail waving his
hand to one or two men on the little steamer
who recognized him and shouted at him. Mrs,

(she refused to be called *La Signora*) Conchas
Especiales, the wife of the great Cuban tobacco
planter, and Mrs. Freebody, stood arm in arm
under the awning, with my husband lying on
the deck near them. Captain Brague and
Eleanor Gander were in the bow together,
(either flirting or concocting mischief, it was
impossible to tell which) and " Paddy " Gander
and I were swinging ourselves by some of those
mysterious ropes that are always so plentiful on
board a yacht. If I had been on the Narragansett boat instead of on the yacht I know that I
should have jumped overboard out of sheer
envy. How salt and cool was the wind which
blew athwart our bows that day ! how clear and
distinct showed the shores by which we sailed !
It was my first big "spree" and I enjoyed it accordingly. Paddy Gander was giving me a
most amusing account of the little artifices
practiced by Nosenberg, a young Hebrew who
was trying to get into society in Newport, and
who went incessantly to a Presbyterian church
thinking that no one would believe that he

could be a convert if that were his faith, when
Captain Brague called to us to come and see his
little invention. This consisted of a roulette
board, chalked out upon the deck, and a tecto-
tum which one of the sailors had made for him
out of a bit of wood. The captain constituted
himself the " bank," and we were all of us soon
absorbed in pushing about the little squares of
cardboard from a game of logomachy which
somehow turned up in the cabin, and other
small articles, representing the heavy stakes
(they were only quarter-dollars) for which we
had agreed to play. Eleanor Gander became
tremendously excited, and, when Mrs. Especiales pulled out a little package of Cuban ciga-
rettes, declared that if she had not learned to
smoke in Cuba it was only because she had
never had the opportunity, and promptly thrust
a cigarette between her audacious little lips. Of
course it became a disastrous wreck; but after
she had had one rolled for her, she puffed away
with much delight. Mrs. Freebody began to
smoke without any ado ; but I declined, because

I was privately afraid of being ill, and I was rather glad I had done so when I saw Eleanor coughing at every third puff. Our game, which was interrupted by this little incident, was resumed with more fervor than ever; and whenever Mr. Langton proposed to have "a little appetizer before lunch," the idea was received with entire acquiescence. I caught myself wondering what the sailors would think of it. After all, there was nothing extraordinary in it. We were living a perfectly natural existence. When the sailors were on shore they played cards and drank spirituous liquors; our game was a little more involved and our "drinks" were "mixed." Our impulses were perfectly natural. We were really free from artificial polish and veneer. We conducted ourselves with sufficient propriety because we had innate ideas on the subject, not because we chose to pay a hypocritical homage to conventional virtue. Such, at least, were my thoughts at the time. As I say, I did smile a little to find myself spread out at full length on a rug, sip-

8

ping a sherry cobbler and laughing at a conversation which owed none of its attractiveness
to covert allusion or sly reference.   But where
was the harm? I had been accustomed to
take not a little pride in my cleverness in man-
aging a conversation so as to steer clear of
people's prejudices and flatter their peculiari-
ties; so as to suggest rather than to speak
plainly and to glide over things personal or
undignified with easy grace; but the people
with whom I now mingled seemed to take no
thought of possible deep feeling, to be utterly
regardless of hidden meanings. They talked
of every thing with the utmost frankness; I
began to think that I had been only stiff where
I thought I had been dignified, and unneces-
sarily prudish where I had supposed myself to
be very elevated in tone.   I never once said to
myself, *Vogue la galère*, and I had no feeling
that I was falling away from righteousness;
I was quite content to think that this was the
proper way of life, and that if Bunyan had not
gone to the Celestial City along this path it

was only because the necessities of his century
had forced upon him a narrower set of ideas.
"Lady Mary was quite right," said I, thinking aloud, just after making some reflections
similar to these.

"What on earth is Mrs. Charter talking
about?" said Paddy Gander. "Mrs. Charter,
your 'lush' has gone to your head I'll be bound.
Why didn't you listen to my story about my
sister Eleanor and the milk-punch?"

"Mrs. Charter is absent-minded? Charter,
that's a doosid bad sign. I'll go bail that your
wife has smashed herself on some London actor.
Plenty of girls have done that, you know."

Eleanor Gander jumped up at this sally from
Katty Langton, and threatened to pour a pitcher
of champagne-cup over his head. Miss Gander
was the young lady who had had a statue made
of Capulet, the handsome young tragedian,
after the pattern of the Belvidere Apollo, and
always had it put on the table when she took
her breakfast. I got a chance to explain presently that I had been thinking of Lady Mary

Wortley Montague's saying, that she had been all over the world and found only two kinds of people—men and women.

"All people *are* alike," said Paddy Gander.

"Not a bit of it," said Captain Brague. "Men are divided into two classes—the men who'll trust you and the men who won't."

"And the girls are divided into two classes—the girls who'll kiss you and the girls who won't," said Paddy, laughing.

"Not for you, you impertinent young man," said Mrs. Freebody.

"Well—which do you mean?"

"I'm an old woman, sir, and I wasn't a girl when you began to go about; but if I had been there would have been an exception. *I* should have boxed your ears."

"Well," said Paddy, "I wish all girls would kiss me."

"Isn't he horrid!" said Eleanor.

You see, at the very first I fell in with people who egged me on, and if I took pleasure in such employment as this, it may be supposed that my liking did not fail for want of supply. By the time we returned to Philadelphia I had come to have a very decided opinion as to the manner in which I wished to amuse myself during the winter. After we had fairly settled down in our country house I began to think Philadelphia stupid and perhaps provincial; but I soon found opportunity to continue my career of gayety.

VI.

THE international cricket match that year was with the Oxford Strollers, a lot of young Oxford graduates who had come over more for fun than for cricket. As I was really fond of the game I went with Penny to the grounds early in the morning, and reaped my reward by having all the Englishmen presented to me before play was called. They went to the bat; and by lunch-time I had thoroughly established myself as the patroness of these sunburned young heroes, and they were promised to me for a garden party. I imparted this welcome intelligence to my girls—(being now a matron, this was the manner in which I spoke of Lotty and Olive)—when I met them at the gate, and drew from them the warmest encomiums. This was after lunch; and presently several of the cricketers returned to my side bestowing themselves on the steps and in the seats of our own men; and just as our gayety was at its height, in walked Mrs. Maples, the hitherto acknowledged queen of cricket matches, looking wonderfully trig and complete in a lovely white cambric, only to find that I had been beforehand with her. All the girls in the grand stand were furiously envious of us already, and our position was emphasized when Mrs. Maples took her seat—for she happened to be directly below us and was unattended save by domestic cavaliers. I could not resist the temptation to rub it in a little. When I looked in the direction of Sir Edward Cover-Poyntz he was talking to Lotty in the most ardent manner. "At Mrs. Charter's garden party there will be dancing, I suppose Miss Hathorne?"

"I suppose so, my lord."

"I say you know, you mustn't call me 'my lord' I'm only Sir Edward."

"But that sounds so—familiar," says Lotty, (the wretch!)

"Then drop the 'Sir,' you know. But will

you give me a dance? Will you promise me
the first and the second and the third—?"

"Goodness, your grace! what will my young
man say?"

"Have you a young man?—do you allow
followers, Mrs. Charter?"

"Which I will not deceive your Royal
Highness," says Lotty, "I have a young man.
How was I to know about you?"

"You ought to have told me sooner—it
wasn't safe? How shall I be able to score now?"
At this point I thought it proper to begin:
"Mrs. Maples," I said, "I am going to have a
a garden party on Saturday for the cricketers
and you must come. Will you? and let me
present Sir Edward Cover- Poyntz." Sir
Edward bowed.

"Mrs. Charter is awfully good to us," said he;
"I hope you'll come to our garden party—it
will be a jolly affair, I vow. I'm going to put
up a wicket and bowl to the ladies."

"Do come," said I sweetly," pray do!" Then
I presented all the other Englishmen about

me, none of whom was at all likely to leave his
occupation, and leaned back in my seat, happy
in the consciousness that Mrs. Maples felt like
a fisherman forced to watch another man hook-
ing the trout out of *his* particular pool.

All through the three days of the match I
stocked my seats with pretty girls, and the
Englishmen declared loudly that I had laid a
trap for them and rendered them totally unfit
for their duties. They demanded an amount
of sympathy, however, entirely out of propor-
tion to their not overwhelming defeat; but
candor compels me to admit that they got it,
and that many girls were so unpatriotic as to
wish them to be victorious. I am afraid to state
the number of reed-birds that Sir Edward was
supposed to have eaten at my garden-party; and
I never saw a man flirt in a more enthusiastic
and determined manner. Nor were his associates far behind him. I myself can testify that
so strongly was I tempted to put myself under
the influence of my own "cedarn alleys" that
I almost forgot that I was, for the first time,

a hostess. But my garden party was a tremendous success. Even the Chinese lanterns commanded admiration.

And now was coming to pass the fulfillment of all my desires. Now I had the enjoyment of all the things for which I had longed as a girl. I had but to lift my hand and the resources of society were open to me. And when I now displayed myself in my true colors society stood amazed. I was no longer Ethel Jones the quiet, the well-mannered, the intelligent, the almost aristocratic—I was Mrs. Charter the fashionable, the dashing, the daring, the unrestrained. I had hardly appeared that winter before the dowagers began to look at me with awful eyes. Many an ample bosom heaved with indignation at the thought that *this* was the girl of whom they, the dowagers, had approved, at whose not-to-have-been-expected good manners they had wondered, whose severe style they had observed with admiration and with whom they had pointed many a moral and adorned many a tale.

"Look," cried their daughters to them again,
"what does your precious Ethel Jones do as
soon as she gets her liberty?" And oh! will
the discerning reader please imagine how little
I cared for serried ranks of dowagers? I could
bear their saying that it showed I had only
married Penny for his money! he did not believe it. And what was my triumph as I
swept into the Assembly *that* year! how different my feelings! With my cheeks rosy and
dimpling, my eyes flashing, the soft and glisten-
ing coils of my hair making my neck show all
the whiter and more slender, the dazzle and
brilliancy of my shoulders and arms shaming
the high dresses of most of the women, never
had I looked so well before! Instead of a
simple white tulle I wore a cream-yellow satin
thick as a board, cut more simply than any tulle
could be, and, with my dozen of bouquets
slung in a string over my free arm, by the time
that I had made half a turn of the room I had
half the men in it at my side. Low neck was
unfashionable that winter; and even Mrs.

Jimmy Maples could only scoff at me for out-
raging the mode; but if the approbation of the
men counts for any thing, fashion was wrong,
terribly wrong! Even Penny himself would
hardly leave my side. I exulted—I triumphed.
Wherever I went, like a comet I carried my
train with me. Nor did I loiter through the
galleries, or hide myself for hours behind the
shrubbery, flirting with one man—my progress
through the galleries was triumphal. Look!
I felt like crying to the other women, can I
not wear diamonds as well as if they had been
handed down to me from my ancestors? Can
I not carry my head as high as do they whose
backbones have been stiffened by hundreds of
family traditions? Such were the pardonable
feelings that agitated me; but I smiled at the
dowagers as sweetly as ever I used to do in my
demure days. I went down to supper still
triumphant with a dozen men disputing over
me, and somewhat to the disgust of Penny, who
wanted to *fêter* me in a corner of the stairs by
ourselves, established myself at one of the little

tables with all my *queue* around me. Just as I
sat down Bran Boullter passed by. I had not
seen much of him during the winter, but now
he turned and asked for a place in my court,
and laughed as loudly as any of my courtiers
while we emptied the bottles of champagne
that they bore boldly off from the supper table.
I had not placed myself where I was from any
ostentatious feelings, and it was only careless
gayety that led me to approve of the frolicsome
humor of my cavaliers. I suppose we made a
great deal of noise, and we certainly sat out
every body else. Several cigars had been
lighted about the dining room before I left it,
and not even a stray ribbon on the stairs kept
my sex company.

Never had there been such a success. I
might almost have thought that I was the
Assembly. I dare say my female readers will
think that my head was easily turned. "If,"
they will say, "every girl who had not much
attention during her first winter were to fancy
that because she had a better time in her

second she was the belle of the season, no one
would be a wall-flower." Very true, young
ladies ; but I assure you I knew how to measure
my own success. What was the meaning of the
constant throng of men about me ; not five men,
not six men, but a dozen, fifteen, twenty? You,
when you go to the Assembly, gather around
you the men of your own set ; when Emily's
latest swain talks to you ten minutes longer
than he does to Emily, your blue eyes gleam
with pleasure ; when, for three turns of the
room, four men are by your side, you look side-
ways at the girls who can boast of only one
man, and he a man of their chance, not of their
choice. You look at them, I say, in scorn, and
you are right. If you have not enough spirit
to enjoy your conquests, you should never be a
warrior. But do you know what is meant by
the height of popularity? Can you imagine
what the feelings would be of a popular song,
a popular novel—your name in every one's
mouth, your form in every one's eye, your qualities in every one's thoughts? My dear girls, I

have reached these heights. The men who spoke
to me, who rushed after me, who were whirled
in the eddies about me were not the men whom
I saw at every party to which I went, with
whom I cracked the same little jokes; they were
of every set, of every sort—callow youths with
budding mustaches, half-afraid, half-valiant,
stately *pères-de-famille*, superior young men
who until now had held themselves aloof,
familiar friends, laughing acquaintances, smirk-
ing foreigners, eager strays from Boston, Baltimore, New York, all bowing, pushing, smiling,
catching up my words, begging for waltzes,
flowers, promenades! This was a cosmopolitan
triumph; this was the gayety of the capital
of the world. I led the stately movement round
the room. I was the most noticeable figure in
all that beautiful array. Frightened debutantes
slipped to their seats awed and wondering;
grisly dowagers frowned in disapproval, and I
felt myself lifted up beyond the possibility of
caring whether it was all happening or not!

After all, I suppose this *is* an exaggerated

view to take of it; but it seems true enough as
I remember it. Certainly after supper I moved
through the German a queen, and reigned over
that part of the evening. Flower after flower
dropped from my bouquets; but still I showed,
—without a ribbon misplaced, without an inch of
my balayeuse torn—the most unflagging dancer,
the most daring and breathless in my whirl. At
last it ended—we left the floor, strewn with
flowers, broken fans, feathers, lace, and rags,
for another year, and sought our carriages and
homes. A moral philospher would comment,
I dare say, on the fact that as we went to bed
many people rose to begin their daily labors.
But what does that prove? If these people were
situated as we are they would keep the same
hours that we do. As I stepped into our hallway
I began humming a waltz. Penny laughed, and,
bundled up as I was, I began to twirl round
again, slipping off my wrap and waving my
arms.

"Don't, my dear, don't, I beg of you," said he
catching me. "If any of the men hear you they'll

storm the house, and insist on finishing the ball here!"

And indeed it was reported the next day that I had been serenaded by a few of the younger men, who, I dare say, had had more champagne than usual; but if such an attention was paid to me, I was unaware of it.

It must not be supposed that I achieved this change of front without protest from any of my friends. Matters had not yet gone far enough for Mrs. Hathorne to give me a formal warning or to dismiss me from her confidence; and I am ashamed to say that I had hardly been near Miss Mayburn since my marriage; but Lotty and Olive both took me to task for deserting my former way of life. On the Sunday after the Assembly, for instance, Captain Brague met me at the church door. I was rather surprised to find him still in town, for the rest of the New York men had gone back on Saturday afternoon; but I was by no means displeased to walk up Walnut Street with him, and if I

9

had not seen Lotty sitting in my window, we might have taken quite a stroll together. I fancied that he did me the honor to be a little vexed at having our *tête-à-tête* interrupted, but I wanted Lotty to see him, so I took him in with me.

"Where's Mr. Temple, Lotty?" said I.

"Oh, my dear, it's too distressing! He's gone to Harrisburgh on business, and this morning we were to have gone out to St. James the Less."

" Faith, Miss Hathorne," said Captain Brague, " distress is mighty becoming to you, then, for you look charming this morning—and one could wish that Mr. Temple was oftener in Harrisburgh."

At this extremely Hibernian speech, Lotty chose to be very angry. It was a little awkward; but the poor captain's meaning was perfectly plain and his intention good; however, the result was, that when I asked him to stay to luncheon, Lotty discovered that she must leave us. This was all the more unfor-

tunate because, as she knew, Penny was not
going to be at home—the remembrance of
which fact, by the way, had caused me some
little cynical amusement, when Lotty spoke of
her distress in her Macy's absence. In a few
years, my dear, I said to myself, you'll be not
only willing, but sometimes glad, to have him
off at a distance. The captain and I sat down
to luncheon together, without much regret for
her departure, probably ; but I refused to walk
with him again in the afternoon. When I met
Lotty the next day her brow had by no means
cleared. I brought her displeasure to a head
immediately, for with great want of tact I
jogged her feelings by telling her that she was
not looking as well as usual.

"Ethel," she cried, "why have you changed
so much ? Yesterday it was that horrid captain who took it upon himself to make comments on my personal appearance ; and to-day
you tell me that I'm going off. I don't mind
your remarks, my dear ; but you are no longer
the Ethel that I used to know. It can't be

only your marriage that has changed you—it's
that New York set and nothing else. Don't be
angry now, Ethel; you know I'm not saying it
for spite. I have been thinking of speaking to
you about it for some time. You don't care
for reading; you take no interest in any feminine employment; all you do is to gad about
and enjoy yourself."

I did not suppose that she said it from spite,
—I thought it was the result of a little temporary bad humor; but all the same, I resented
it, and, I am sorry to say, I spoke my mind.
After a woman is married she is less willing to
receive the criticism and advice, however well-
meant it may be, of her fellows. It does not
matter how expansive she may have been as a
girl; contact with masculine habits of mind
seems to affect her. Of course, with some women the reason is plain enough. Their husbands are their oracles, and they will tolerate
no other judgments than their's. But I considered that Lotty spoke injuriously of my
New York friends, and I stood up for them;

and I regret to confess that we both became slightly heated. She instanced to me what Macy said, and of course I promptly retorted with what Penny thought; the result of which was that we both got worse opinions of the man of each other's choice, and no good was done to anybody. Her remonstrances effected very little. I had chosen my way of life; and having set my hand to the plow, I did not care to look back. I may have given the impression, by what I have said in regard to the Assembly of that year, that I still chronicled my doings and struck a standard of enjoyment —but such was not the case. I never came home saying to myself that I had had a "perfect time." No married woman of my then caliber would allow chance to have anything to do with her enjoyment. Girls permit themselves to be affected by extraneous circumstances. They cast up their accounts and carry their invitations, their admirers, and their various adventures, to profit and loss; they carefully calculate their capital and keep a watchful eye on their investments; but we married women who are, so to speak, capitalists, are above that. I cared little where I went. My nerves were never strung by expectation, my appetite never cloyed by satiety nor deadened by want of success; I went from ball to ball, from dinner to dinner, from theater party to theater party, often ignorant until a few hours before the event as to where I was going. I only knew I must be going somewhere.

As a consequence of this frame of mind I lost all desire to maneuver and never found it necessary to assert myself in any particular way. People came to me. If they did not—so much the worse for them. I never troubled my head about them. Mrs. Jimmy Maples soon discovered that I was now entirely innocent of any feelings of rivalry towards her, and very sensibly made up her mind that it would be much better for us to amuse ourselves together than for her to undertake against me hostilities in which she would have to fight a desperate battle in order to triumph and in which she could not even have the satisfaction of being defeated. Accordingly Mr. Latitude remarked that there was a pair of us ; and that if we couldn't manage to make Rome howl nobody else could. I rather wondered at his saying that, for I did not think that I behaved badly at all.

Of course my reading had to take as good care of itself as it could. Lotty used to talk a good deal about " keeping up " her French and German, but when I had time to pick up a book I generally threw it down if it wasn't amusing. I kept up my French, I suppose. I read Gustave Droz and similar writers; but I must confess that I was extremely shocked by one of the later novels of the author of that very sentimental Romance of a Poor Young Man ; and I did not read any French for some time afterwards. As for music, one went to the Opera for conversation ; and nobody now ever thought of asking *me* to join a Shakespeare class.

VII.

AS the year grew on I noticed a change in my disposition for which I was puzzled to account. Formerly I had been charmed to receive Penny's little attentions. It was very comfortable and cozy to drive home in our snug little coupé with his arm around me, to laugh at his foolish little speeches, and to make equally foolish ones in return. At first I thought it must be the natural waning of the honeymoon that caused a cessation of my pleasure in these trifles ; but I soon perceived that the cause lay deeper than that. Was it propriety that led me to shrug my shoulders impatiently, (though I don't wish it to be supposed that I ever let Penny see that I did it,) when he stroked my hair or pressed my fingers? That suggestion was absurd, of course. It was strange that what had seemed quite appropriate while my views had been more conventionally elevated should appear out of keeping now that my theories had become simplified. I was to blame of course, for not setting myself to discover the true explanation of this; but I was content to find myself growing to be extremely independent of my husband and to take a very composed view of our relations. I decided that as long as I performed my duties no more could be expected of me. As to what were my duties I did not take much trouble to consider ; as none oppressed me very considerably it may be agreed, if you like, that I had none. If it was my duty to dress well, that I did with a calm sense of the superiority of my talents ; if it was equally my duty to entertain well, this and similar duties I fulfilled in a like spirit. Penny certainly seemed to be well pleased. He went to his club, he dined out, he never worried me as to what I was going to do during the day or bothered me at night for a *resumé* of my adventures ; and I know that I gave him just as little cause for complaint on that score. He *would* be affec-

tionate, and to that I was resigned, though I
could not help thinking that it would be better
if the feeling were mutual. Still we were together a good deal, though Mr. Latitude did
say that we reminded him of two doves—in different forests; and I'm sure it was never said of
me as it used to be of Mr. Latitude's sweet
tempered sister, that my service had to be of
plate because I broke all my china over my husband's head. We used to have very jolly little
evenings towards the end of Lent, and in the
early summer. A good many people used to
drop in quietly of an evening. Penny got himself a silver grill and somewhere or other picked
up an abominable little book, 'The Bar
Tender's Guide,' with which he was highly
pleased, and by the aid of which he used
to compound mixtures which, to give them
their due, were often nectareous. I admit
that the family next door to us went away
on account of what they called our scandalous
behavior; as they used to nearly kill me by
playing a parlor organ at nine o'clock in the

morning, I cannot say that I felt the blow particularly.

Our most frequent visitors were Mrs. Jimmy Maples, Belmont Lascham, Jack Newmarket and Captain Brague. Belmont Lascham and Jack Newmarket were great horsemen. They were forever talking on matters equestrian; they belonged to innumerable Hare-and-Hound Clubs, Hunts, Meets, and so forth; their calendar depended on such great feasts as the Baltimore races; when they stood in my drawing room windows on Sunday morning they criticised the horses and not the people who passed; and when there was nothing else going on they ran about to country fairs and not unfrequently rode races themselves at such places by way of keeping their hands in. Of my old friends I saw very little. Olive had become very religious, after the death of poor Willy Woodburn, who killed himself while out shooting, and to whom she had been engaged since they were children, and she now gave up her whole time to sewing-classes, Sunday schools and other charitable employments; and as for Lotty, she was too much occupied with her approaching marriage to think of any thing else. The only one of my old friends of whom I saw any thing was, curiously enough, Bran Boullter. Bran appeared to me to have changed a good deal. He was by no means so uniformly gay as he had been. His humor was often wild and a little dangerous, and I noticed that he was sometimes depressed. Report said, moreover, that he drank a good deal; I myself, had often seen him with flushed face and tumbled hair, talking in an excited manner. Once or twice I heard it whispered that some girl had treated him very badly; but I had no suspicion as to who it could be. We were very good friends, but, on account of his changed temperament, I did not take as much pleasure in his society as I formerly had done, and I rather preferred the jovial manner and careless laugh of Captain Brague. Then, too, Bran made a shift, once or twice, to get me to sympathize with his afflictions. One afternoon, I remember, we had made up a party

to go out to our country house and spend Sunday—agreeing, as Bran had put it, that we
would fly from the dark and noisome by-ways
of the city to the green fields and the sunny
champaign. It had been arranged that Bran
should drive me out in the dog-cart, every body
else going in the drag. Bran had been so very
delightful before the excursion, making outrageous verses about seeking for modest violets
and quaffing the frothing vintage of the bovine,
that I promised myself a very jolly time with
him ; but as soon as we started I noticed that
his humor had changed. He scarcely spoke at
all as we drove up to the Park; and I began to
think that I should have to amuse myself with
the scenery. Quite contented with this idea, I
was leaning a little away from him and looking up
the wooded slopes of the Schuylkill, now faintly
green, when he suddenly turned towards me and
asked me, rather abruptly, if I was not bored.

" Not at all," said I. " To tell you the truth
I was looking at the river and had almost forgotten your existence."

He turned away and flicked his whip at the leader, who was dancing a little; then he looked at me very earnestly.

"Mrs. Charter," said he, "I am in a bad way. What ought a fellow to do when he's in a bad way?"

I must say I felt rather aggrieved, at first. Why should people have afflictions? Why could not every body take things easily, as I did? I was willing to be sorry for poor Bran, but what could I do for him? Such were my rather selfish reflections; but in a minute or two I began to feel some of my old fondness for him, and, vaguely wondering whether it was about some girl or about some other kind of a scrape that he was going to tell me, I laid my hand on his arm, without thinking much about it, and said:

"I'm awfully sorry to hear it. Why do you let yourself think of it?"

He looked at my glove and then back at me, and said, with a curious laugh;

"You could never guess what it is about."

"I don't know," said I, with a smile that was meant to make him more cheerful, "I might guess."

"Perhaps you'd rather guess it than have me tell you." His eyes gleamed a little, as if he wanted me to say that I would rather guess, but as I found, with a little sense of shame, that I did not care sufficiently about it to do that, I merely answered that he had better tell me.

"By Jove!" said he, "I have it. You shall find it out."

"I hate mysteries," said I. "What is it—stocks?"

"That's very good," he replied. "Yes—I did take stock in—in something. Look here—if a fellow should hesitate about doing something, and then see another fellow go in for the same thing and nearly succeed—don't you think the first fellow ought to prick up his ears and go in himself?"

"Why, yes," said I. "'He either fears his fate too much,'—you know the rest."

"Hah!" His exclamation was quick and deep-toned.

"I think it would be better for me to drown my sorrows in the bowl—a jolly sight better!"

Again I felt a little of my old softness towards him, and I said, in a sympathizing tone:

"Don't do that—Bran."

He gave the horses a couple of cuts, which made them jump horribly, and then pretended to be entirely taken up with them.

"I don't altogether believe it's a girl," said I to myself. "Dear me, I hope it's nothing disgraceful." And on that very evening, as I was standing by myself on the piazza, enjoying the first soft breezes of the young season, he came up up and took my hand with something of a clutch. "Shall I tell you about that now?" said he.

I didn't mind his taking my hand, though I did not think it was necessary for him to squeeze it, and, as I was in a somewhat sentimental mood just then, I rather fancied the idea of consoling him and being a ministering angel; so I said softly:

" Yes, if you like."

But he hesitated, and then, muttering slowly that he had not yet made up his mind, he went away again.

After that was it remarkable that I decided that his sorrows were a little of a bore? Why on earth should people be tragic? I was not tragic. I was rarely out of temper—even with my dressmakers. So I settled it with myself that Captain Brague was the man of our little circle who best suited my disposition. Belmont Lascham and Jack Newmarket were very devoted to me, and were awfully proud of me on horseback; but they were a little narrow-minded, and then they had a way of talking of their achievements that I didn't much care about. To be sure Paddy Gander and the captain never made any secret of the number of their bottles of champagne, or of the amount of their losses; but then they never pretended that such things were any special credit to them and never mentioned them unless they were germane to the conver-

10

sation; but I must admit that they frequently were so.

It is unnecessary, and, indeed, it would be tiresome;for me to recount all my adventures during the second year of my married life. The tenor of my days was even enough. The course of my doings may easily be imagined. In the summer we went to Newport again, and continued our career of simple and unpretentious gayety. I know that those two adjectives have an ironical appearance, but I use them advisedly. Our gayety was simple, for it was absolutely unmixed with any foreign element of any kind; unless perhaps a little soda water in the morning for the men is to be considered an incident foreign to gayety; and we certainly never pretended to be any better than any body else, though we possibly were allowed to be faster. I sometimes used to think that I should like to have a little conversation with some of the people who deprecated our doings and condemned our way of life. " My dears," I should have said to them, " what is your complaint? My friends and I certainly don't interfere with you. We enjoy life, no doubt; but then consider, we are in a position to do so, and we act on principle as much as you do. Only think how many things we have that you have not. Of course I don't speak of money—I mean, for instance, good taste, and appreciation, and health, and a certain amount of animal spirits. Do you think we cannot enjoy the natural beauties about us? What nonsense! Instead of carping at us, come and pay us a visit. You will find us very hospitable, unaffected in our manners, and willing to be fond of you if you please us. We'll take you driving in delightful vehicles, we'll tell you exceedingly amusing anecdotes, we'll make you nearly die of laughing when we expose to you the eccentricities of your relations and of ours as well; we'll give you toothsome things to eat and drink, delicacies of which you have never dreamed, perhaps; you shall play charming games, have your own way in every thing, and say any thing you like of us to our

faces. I assure you we are charitable and
very liberal-minded. For see—we don't object
to you, though goodness knows your serious-
ness is *assez bête;* and if you do visit us you
shall be as Puritanical as you please and we'll
not murmur. *Que voulez-vous?*" ·Something
of this sort I did say to Lotty who came to us
with her husband for a few days in August;
but they went away soon, thinking, I believe,
that they didn't get enough of each other's
society; "though goodness knows," I said to
myself at the time, "if they didn't want to
racket about with us they needed only to have
said so."

But oh, how agreeable was my life! If to be
lacking several things, such as rocs' eggs and
private Pullman cars, and a coronet, and a company of soldiers to ride about with you, is to
fall short of absolute happiness, then I was unhappy; but if contentment is the test of happiness then was I happy to a degree. I deputed
all my unattractive work, and did well every
thing that I wished to do; and therein lies the

true secret of happiness, if you are only wise
enough to wish for the right thing. Otherwise
your career will be cut short by Nemesis, who
will come down on you, just like the fairy god-
mothers in the old fables.

But I never became too paganized. I spent
my time in idleness it is true; I left undone
most of the things that I ought to have done, and
I did many things that I ought not to have done,
and the rest of my time was taken up in doing
things that made not much difference one way
or the other. I entered with perfect equanimity
into discussions which only engaged the notice
of my companions by their doubtful character;
I viewed with toleration the errors of some of
my associates; indeed, I remember that when,
on one disastrous occasion, Penny, in company
with a good many other men, succumbed to the
effects of a grand dinner, I was more amused
than horrified; I adopted several masculine
habits and ways of thought; and, in short, I
suppose I came to think that there was no
reason why a woman should be any better than

a man, or entertain herself in any smaller variety
of ways. In the pleasures of dress I was an
epicure of the first water. I treated the various
members of my body almost as sentient beings
and bestowed as much thought on a stocking
or a petticoat as upon the skirt of a ball dress.
But I never took baths of perfumed milk, for
instance, nor practiced any of the other Oriental
luxuries in which many women indulge themselves. And if I was too luxurious, I was at
least refined. At any rate it is rather degrading
to talk about it. It is a great pity that we are
not all stirred solely by angelic emotions and
all made of Dresden china.

Of course it was by gradual degrees that I
arrived at such a state of mind. I have endeavored to make that state of mind entirely
plain to the reader and to point out to her how
insensibly I came to adopt the opinions which
I then held. I hope it will be borne in mind
that the little sketch which I am writing is intended to have a distinct moral. I am now approaching its catastrophe; and I am anxious

that my actions may not be misunderstood. I do not wish to be thought either too culpable or too innocent. Let no woman think that it would be impossible for her moral sensibilities to become as blunted as were mine ; and let no man conclude that my powers of recuperation were still vigorous because I was not really as perverted as I make myself out to have been. My own opinion is that I stopped just in time.

VIII.

IT was about Christmas of the year of which I have last been speaking—I hope the reader's ideas of my chronology are not utterly disarranged—that my views arrived at the extreme which I have indicated. About two months later came the catastrophe.

It was Mrs. Maples who suggested to me the idea of going to the Young Maennerchor Carnival on our own private account. I had fully intended to go, though I had only thought of going in a party ; but I at once approved of her scheme. For of course I agreed that it would be much more amusing for us to go together with a single cavalier and attack not only the world of our acquaintance, but also our familiar and intimate circle. " My dear," said I, " if we can manage it carefully enough we'll have all the men, and especially my husband, stunned and frantic." And I laughed with delight when I thought of the manner in which I would perplex the wits of my poor Penny, whose perceptions were never at any time extraordinarily acute. The first step was to decide on a cavalier; the rest to arrange our plans.

I may pause for a moment to say that it must not be supposed that when I have spoken of our *little* set that I have meant to imply that my field of operations had become limited. I was still at the height of popularity and success —as much quoted and flattered as ever. Yet it is true that I did not touch all points within my reach, and I dare say that I might soon have lost my fame and become wholly identified with the pleasure-seeking set which most I affected.

Thus though I could, at that time, have picked out almost any man in society to assist Mrs. Maples and myself in our little adventure, I turned over in my mind only the men of whom I have lately been speaking. Mrs. Maples seemed rather to wish for Captain Brague, but I thought it would not be quite politic for me to

undertake such an adventure in his company.
For I knew, though it affected me very little,
that we had been considerably talked about.
It was flagrantly unjust, for the captain and I
had never become even intimate, though we
had been together a good deal, and the only
fault that ought to have been found with us by
society was that we neither of us had any thing
particular to do; it made no difference that we
sometimes preferred to do it together. Even
my mother appeared to be anxious about me
on his account. She was now living by herself
in a comfortable little house, my sister, (who
had in the most ungrateful manner refused to
take advantage of the opportunities which I in
the endeavor to do my duty by her, had offered
to her), having left the maternal roof to live in
Lancaster! Actually, she married a farmer!
My mother, accordingly, had more time to be-
stow on me—when she could catch me—and in
our conversations she exhibited a good deal of
uneasiness about my way of life. "You are
too rapid, my dear Ethel," said she. "Such a

pace will ruin your health, if you don't take care, and there's always the chance that you may get into some other kind of trouble." But I met her objections with an unanswerable argument when I pointed out to her the difference between my sister's affairs and mine, and asked her which of her daughters she considered to be the most fortunate.

So, as I say, I determined not to call upon the captain for assistance, and agreed without any particular demur to Mrs. Maples' next suggestion,—which was of Bran Boullter. As to our plans, they were easily framed, and the only thing to do was to carry them out carefully. I managed to be free on the evening of the ball in such a manner as not to run the chance of arousing Penny's suspicions; when he asked me in a perfunctory manner if I did not wish to go, I hesitated just long enough to make him think that I really did not care about it; and of course there was no difficulty in keeping my costume out of his sight. Emma Maples and I had agreed to dress alike in order

the better to be able to confuse our friends;
and we fixed on white dominos with tasseled
hoods and white silk vizards as our costume.
Bran Boullter was to call for Emma and then
go to my mother's house for me.

But on the evening of the appointed day,
when, after having seen Penny go off with his
cigar, I had gone to my mother's and was sitting
in the parlor waiting, I was inclined to be sorry
that I had not agreed to go with the captain.
For on the afternoon of that very day something had occurred which had considerably
enlightened me as to the reason of Bran's
changed condition. He met me in Walnut
street and walked home with me. It was a
gorgeous afternoon; the russet bar of the sun-
set glowed at the end of the vista of the street,
fading off into the cold pale blue of the wintry
sky; the heaps of snow and the darkening
pavements about us were beginning to chill the
air which had caught a little glow of cheerful-
ness during the day from the glittering sun;
dark through the leafless trees in the square

moved the hurrying forms of workmen, and the crunch of their feet on the snow sounded · crisp and strong. I was glad to be walking briskly against the empty cold; the little patches of dusted snow on which I trod seemed elastic and invigorating. When we came indoors out of the falling darkness, I pulled off my seal-skin coat quickly and ran to the soft coal fire in the back drawing-room, and stood looking into its elfin blaze, shading my glowing cheek with benumbed hands. Presently I began to rub my hands over the heat.

"Are your hands cold?" said Bran; there was a deep tremble in his voice.

"Yes" said I.

Without saying any thing more he took one of my hands in both of his and began stroking it slowly. I looked up at him quickly. The room was unlighted save by the fire, and as he leaned against the mantel the firelight flickered on his face. A sudden apprehension took· possession of me—his intent gaze must mean

something. "Is it possible," said I—my hand
still lay passive in his—"is it possible that—
that—"

"That you are the cause of all my troubles?"
said he. "Yes, it is."

I looked away from him and into the fire.
My first impulse had been to draw my hand
away instantly; but unfortunately I hesitated.
I really did not sufficiently think of the situation. Bran's presence that afternoon had somehow affected me. I had been delighted to see
him when he stopped; it was like old times;
I felt like his cousin, his old comrade, and the
old fondness for him returned, as it would every
now and then. All the way up the street I had
been lightly remembering the old days; and
now I forgot myself and delayed the instant
of reason and reproof. But the fire gave me
no counsel. I watched it for a little while in
silence, knowing that his eyes were on me all
the time. Poor boy, poor boy! So I had
been to blame for all his unhappiness! I turned
again presently and looked at him steadily.

"You should not say this to me," I said. "You must go."

He dropped my hand and left me.—So, as I said, I was very thoughtful as I sat in my mother's little parlor and waited·for him and Emma Maples. My chief trouble was to fix the exact amount of my own responsibility, but the more I thought the more it seemed to be reduced; and though at first I had felt almost as soft-hearted about him as on that eventful evening when I had refused him, finally, becoming somewhat impatient as he and Emma Maples still delayed, I decided that if any body was to blame Bran Boullter was; for I had given him absolutely no encouragement, and if his foolish speeches to me while we drove through the Park together had been based upon the supposition that I was encouraging Captain Brague why he deserved the additional unhappiness which he would now receive from having mistaken my meaning when I told him not to fear his fate too much. He need not run after me unless he wants to, said I; and of course he

must do so no longer. I was really sorry for
the poor boy ; I seemed fated to destroy his
happiness ; but I clearly was not to blame.
While I was trying to think over the best way
to reprove poor Bran—Dear me ! what an unnecessary amount of trouble I seemed to be having—the door bell rang, and presently he came
in alone !

"Where's Emma? where's Mrs. Maples?"
said I.

"She can't go," said he. "Here's a note
from her."

I took the note—she simply said that she had
a bad headache and could not go ; she was
awfully sorry and begged me to enjoy myself
without thinking of her. I mused over the let-
ter for a little while. It was my duty, I supposed, considering the circumstances, to give up
the expedition. I had at last succeeded in jus-
tifying my going at all on the argument that
Mrs. Maples' presence would do away with all
possibility of a suspicion on Bran's part that I
did not mean to be angry with him. But now?

Well, after all, what harm could there be in going? I had quite made up my mind to be very serious with him, and in the mean time there was no reason why I should lose any fun just because he had chosen to behave foolishly. When I had thus decided I looked up and said calmly:

"Then I suppose we shall have to go without her. What a pity she is not well." A slight movement passed over his features. I could not detect its import—"Dear me," I said to myself, "I hope he is not going to give me any more trouble! At all events I can treat him like a stick of wood, and if I am impassive, what can he do?" All at once I remembered that my domino was out in the carriage, and I stopped for a moment; at the end of which time I had decided that my costume was too conspicuous for me, and that I could very well make use of an old black domino and mask which I had once had for some girlish frolic, and which I knew was somewhere among my mother's belongings. In a

11

few minutes I had found it, leaving Bran with
my mother, who had in the meantime come
down-stairs; I slipped it on in the vestibule,
and presently we were off.

I felt quite a little pleasurable quiver of excitement as I jumped out of the carriage and
passed up the steps of the Academy of Music.
A gaping crowd of idlers stood about; curious
looking women and absolutely extraordinary
men were entering the building at the same
time with myself; this was indeed delightful.
I was soon on the floor, and, holding in one
hand a knot of jacqueminot roses which Bran
had produced at the last moment, and which I
thought it would complicate matters least to
accept carelessly, I took a couple of turns
around the room with him to get an idea of how
I should begin for myself. Somehow or other
the roofing over of the pit did not give the
effect of as much size as I had expected; but
there were throngs of people. We were too
late for the entrance of King Carnival; but
plenty of gaudily dressed men of extremely

Teutonic countenance helped to give somewhat of the appearance of a full masked ball. It was curious to notice how differently different people regarded the affair. The honest German burghers came with their families, seeming to find nothing improper in bringing them. I saw several small girls with fair hair and tinsled dresses moving about in the crowd apparently perfectly at home. Up in the second gallery sat quite a number of folk who looked as sober as if they were at a lecture; in the proscenium boxes were knots of women draped as blackly as possible, who talked together mysteriously and made little sallies on to the floor guarded by pickets and vedettes of anxious cavaliers; unattached maskers ran about here and there, teasing one man, flying from another; bravely dressed women scarcely masked at all sat about in the parquette circle; and the men were every where. Oh, the men! I had heard tales, and I had had a general idea that they went on the sly; but to see the literary young men, and the sober middle-aged married men, and the grave

lawyers, and the stiff-necked physicians actually
there in the flesh was too delightful! I soon
cast loose from Bran's arm, and, telling him to
keep a general eye on my movements, but not
to appear to belong to me, started off on a
career of amusement. I caught old Mr. Pelican
waddling about in huge delight, laughing and
gobbling. I tapped him on the shoulder and
whispered to him that his grand-daughter was
following him in a blue mask, and that she was
going to bring his wife after him at half-past
ten. I made out Letty Risquict through her
disguise, and nearly scared her to death by
telling her that Johnny Woodcock (he was
crazy about her at that time) had found out
that she had come, and was in an awful state,
swearing vengeance on the man who had
brought her. I left Mr. Latitude in speechless
astonishment, having asked him with tender
solicitude if he had been careful about his
flannels, and had put his pills and his powders
in his pocket; and oh how I enjoyed myself
with Penny! I came upon him quite suddenly

in the middle of the room. He was surveying
the scene with a look of thorough enjoyment
on his face and a flower in his button-hole. I
tapped him on the shoulder.

" Well, my dear," said he, " and what do you
want? "

" I know you," said I, in squeaky tones.

" Do you? Well, I'll warrant I know you."

" You are Mrs. Charter's husband," said I,
and turned as if to run away. As I expected,
he was after me in a moment, laughing and a
little red in the face, not knowing whether to
be displeased or amused.

" You certainly are not Mr. Charter's wife,"
he said. " Take my arm and see if I don't
know who you are."

We slipped out together into the corridor.

" Now take care what you say to me," said I.
" How do you know that I am not in Mrs.
Charter's confidence? "

" I know you would be too honorable to
repeat to her what I am going to say to you,"
he replied. " I know you pretty well."

"Yes?"

"And I am very glad to have a chance to speak to you in this way, for now I can tell you what the cold atmosphere of society in which we have formerly met has always frozen on my lips."

"Ah!" said I.

"Yes—often have I seen you in the—er—the giddy whirl, looking like Aurora—"

"Goodness!" said I. "You know I am a blonde!"

"I told you I knew you," said he. "Can I not see your eyes? Don't I know your voice? Yes, often have I seen you, beautiful as the day, and—and the sight of you has almost floored me." This last was rather unpoetical.

"Ah, Mr. Charter," said I, pressing his arm, "this is very dangerous. Alas, I ought not to have come with you."

"Was the temptation so great?" said he, squeezing my arm in return till it was almost black and blue, and gazing at me with the most egregious pair of sheep's eyes. I only sighed.

" Don't you remember what I said to you the last time we met—at—?" this was rather deep for Penny.

"At dinner?" said I. "When you gave me some almonds and asked me if knew what the gift of an almond meant in Arabia?"

("Good Lord!" I could almost hear him saying to himself—" to whom did I say that? I must have been coming it rather strong.")

" I told you that I did not know," said I. " I said it coldly, but I do know. I was afraid to say I did, for I feared that my feelings would overpower me." And I sighed again.

This last touch entirely overcame him, and for half an hour I amused myself by making him commit every description of folly. Though I could not make him tell me who he thought I was, still I guessed his suspicions, and that was something. He begged me for a rose till I began to think he was crazy; and, in short, he "gave himself away" as completely as the faithful heart of a wife could possibly have wished. I finally tore myself away from him, hav-

ing secured his *boutonnière*, which I proposed to
display to him the next time I caught him spoon-
ing on a bud.   Not all my adventures, however,
were of a pleasing description.   I was rather
taken aback by the very rude manner in which
I was accosted in the corridor by a perfectly
strange man, and I suppose I must have showed
some agitation, for he asked me in a discontented tone whether I had any business there and
told me that it served me right for being in
such a place.   There too, I met Johnny Woodcock who really had harbored some vague
suspicions of Letty's doings—he was in an awful
temper, at any rate—and he marched up to me
and gave me a positive lecture on my injudicious behavior.

I came very near losing my temper when he
told me that he considered it his duty to re-
monstrate with a woman whom he plainly saw
was very much out of place at the Maennerchor,
for his remonstrances were by no means mild;
but I remembered his jealousy and the excellent
cause that the poor boy had to lose his head,

and, instead of begging Bran to come to my
assistance, only told Mr. Woodcock, in a tone of
mockery, that he need not disquiet himself for
I was not Letty and I did not think she was in
the building; to which taunt he replied that he
should now make it his business to find out who
I was. I slipped away from him, then, for I did
not care to be quarreling.

My excitement was cooled a little, every now
and then, moreover. The affair was *bête* in the
pauses. The tobacco of which some of the
men were redolent was awful—I knew too well
myself what good tobacco was—and the tipsi-
ness of others suggested the police station
rather than a club dining-room, which last I
suppose I should not have minded so much.
Taking it all in all I was enjoying myself desperately; but I could not help feeling the shock
of meeting, every once in a while, with somebody who thought the affair perfectly innocent
or who insisted on making it horribly vulgar. I
could not feel that I was continually misbehaving
myself, nor could I feel that when I did mis-

behave I was misbehaving with good taste. So
I determined to cease the roguish little passages
at arms with the men who crossed my course,
and the delightful teasing of my friends, to
come away from the dear attraction of impropriety and to go home. I knew very well that
the ball would be, well, Pandemonium, later on,
and I very much.wished to stay it out ; but I
told myself that only one or two little misgiv-
ings had so far marred my pleasure, and that it
would be better to go away while still on good
terms with my entertainment. So I made a
sign to Bran and told him that I wanted him to
get the carriage. He pondered for a moment,
and then said :

" I say, it's still quite early. Don't you think
you'd like to have a little supper before you go
home ? "

" I will get some supper at home," said I.
" You shall come with me. Though—let me
think a minute."

I hesitated, not because I minded taking him
home with me, but because another idea had

occurred to me. I made up my mind without
much difficulty. Yes, I would do it—and, oh
well, it really wasn't a case of *Vogue la galère.* I
had seen so little of Bran during the evening,
he had been so calm and well-behaved—(possibly
because it was still early)—that it wasn't worth
my while to be on my guard. " I suppose I
ought to go home," I reflected, " but after all,
what difference can it make ? And then it will
finish off my evening very comfortably, and it
will be quite Venetian—or quite Queen Anne ! "
so I said to Bran.

" I want you to do something for me. I want
you to take me to a men's restaurant. I want
to see what it is like. Will you ? "

"Well," said he, with deliberation, " I will.
But we'll have to get a table to ourselves in one
of the smaller rooms, or something of that sort,
you know."

I rather wished that Emma Maples had been
with me ; but I acquiesced, and he went to call
the carriage.

Just as he came back to the vestibule where

I was waiting I lifted the bunch of roses, which
I still held in my hand, to my left shoulder, and
then, on an idle impulse, I took a hair pin and
fastened them there, patting them, and pressing
them to my domino.   Suddenly I noticed Captain Brague looking at me very intently, and it
just occurred to me that I had forgotten him !
I had intended to find out for whom he took
me.   He had been watching me narrowly all the
evening and, indeed, had been following me
about the Academy in a curious manner ; and
I was quite convinced that he had some special
interest in me.   If he thought I was some other
woman I could personate her; if he suspected
me of being myself *tant mieux !*   I could lead
him away from that suspicion and then get him
to talk about me.   So, as I say, I was rather
put out to find that I had missed the accom-
plishment of this plan.   For a moment I hesitated as to whether I should not stay and have
it out with him ; but I reflected that it would
be too much trouble to make it plain to Bran
why I had so signally favored the other, so I

gave it up. "I must hurry however!" said I to myself, for the captain was making straight for me, with eager eyes and looking as if he had a claim on me. "Yes" I continued, "it's too late now." So I took Bran's arm and made him walk rather quickly through the door. Numbers of curious people were lounging about; as we brushed past them I turned to look for the captain. He was following us. "Too late, my gallant friend," said I, and waved my hand to him. At the moment that I did this I saw Penny, also looking at me somewhat eagerly. He was close by my side.

"Good night," he said to me. "That is you, is it?"

"Oh yes," said I. "Come along!"

And I tripped down the steps and as Bran shut the door of the carriage I fancied I caught a glimpse of the captain on the steps of the Academy, looking after us irresolute.

In a few minutes the carriage stopped, and I saw that we were in front of a well-known restaurant quite near to the Academy. Bran jumped out quickly and I followed him with some satisfaction. One or two men who were standing on the steps, took their cigars from their mouths, puffing surprised clouds of smoke into the frosty air, and stared at me deliberately. Bran led the way into a little waiting room.

"Wait here a moment," said he, "while I go look up a waiter and find out about a table."

"But I want to go through the large rooms," said I. "I want to see the men, you know. I'm dying to find out what they're up to."

"I understand," said Bran. "But I'll make arrangements for our supper first."

So off he went. I sat down for an instant in a chair near the door of the *salle d'attente*, highly amused with its stiffly gorgeous chairs, its extraordinary wall-paper and its filigree looking-glass. It ought to have been Queen Anne, I thought to myself, I would make a famous Sacharissa—though my domino isn't quite right for the character. How delightful it would be if Bran were only clad in—well, say in the disguise of a highwayman; or in satin small clothes, silk stockings, a cocked hat and a tie-wig! How well he would look in them! Full of such thoughts I jumped up and went to the glass to see how I looked in a vizard.

Suddenly I heard a noise behind me. I saw in the glass the face of Captain Brague, who was looking into the room. Good heavens! he had followed me! Before I could turn he had rushed quickly to me, and had clasped me fondly about the waist. Was he tipsy? He certainly was, by his way of speech; he spoke confidently and quickly: —

"Sure, why didn't you let me know before that it was you, my dear?—I beg your pardon, but you've been so tantalizing this evening. I misdoubted it was you. Why did you come away with Boullter? Are you angry with me? Did I misunderstand the signal? My dear girl!—"

I had loosened my mask while looking into the glass; and now, to my dismay, as I struggled to get away from Captain Brague, I gave it a push—and it dropped off upon the floor.

"There goes your mask," cried he. "Sure it's you and no mistake. Let me look at you—"

In spite of all I could do he caught sight of my face—I had not dared to speak for fear he should recognize my voice—and as I felt his arm relax and heard him give a quick exclamation I knew that he had recognized me. I lifted my head; flushed and angry I was beginning to chide him; when I saw that his face wore the most extraordinary expression,—a mixture of surprise and bewildered horror; and while he gazed at me with blank amaze the look of horror seemed to deepen as his eyes turned towards the door. I followed his look and saw, standing in the doorway, the very picture of sudden rage—my husband! As I turned to look at him, Penny came forward and grasped me by the wrist.

"So," he said. "It was *you!* First with Boullter—and now I find you with that Irishman."

He gave my wrist a sudden swing and pushed

me away from him. I remember that I thought
at the time—for I was not sufficiently mistress
of the situation to occupy myself with thinking
what I ought to be doing,—that it was exactly
the gesture with which I had seen a hundred
tenors and *jeunes premiers* fling from them an
equal number of soprani and heroines; and I
was really rather amused at the thought. I
wondered what was coming next—and mechanically put my wrist to my mouth. Penny
stood looking at me for a moment. He was
evidently a little *gris*, and his hat was pushed
down over his head. He must have followed
me round from the ball only an instant behind
Captain Brague. What bad luck that they
both should have found me! I heard Captain
Brague begin to say something in an excited
voice. I think he said that he didn't know it
was Mrs. Charter—but I still looked at Penny
—who scowled at me a moment longer, and
then, with what I suppose was a muttered oath,
shook his head with a sort of impulse of rage
and rushed away. Then I comprehended, for

the first time, what it all meant. I had just time to reflect that I was thankful that Bran had not come in while Penny was there—and then I fainted.

THE explanation of it all was simple enough. Emma Maples was at the bottom of the whole affair. She and Captain Brague had been having a most desperate and unsuspected flirtation, and she had been unable to give up the idea of going to the Maennerchor with him. Consequently she had arranged with him to meet her at the ball, thinking that she would run less risk of detection, and had told him that she would wear a black domino with a knot of Jacks on her left shoulder. She had pretended to me that she was going with me, and had written at the last moment so as not to arouse my suspicions. Then, after all, just as she was about to start out, her brother-in-law came after her with the news that her sister had fallen down-stairs and broken her leg. She could not communicate with Captain

Brague; and affairs so arranged themselves
that he took me for her, but did not like to
accost me while I still carried the roses in my
hand. Consequently he had felt bound to follow me when I did give what he supposed was
the signal for which he had been waiting; and,
as for my husband, his actions are easily understood. Moreover, the restaurant being but
a short distance from the Academy, and our
driver being forced to go slowly, on account of
the snowy streets and the numerous vehicles
about the building, my two swains had been
able to watch my carriage and to keep up with
it without much trouble.

It is scarcely necessary to remark that I had
involved myself in very serious difficulties. I
have said that just before I fainted, I thanked
my stars that Penny had gone before Bran
came back; but after I had come to myself
again, which I did almost immediately, I fancy,
I was rather sorry that Penny had not stayed
to see me swoon, after all. For it might have
brought him round—and then every thing might

have been explained then and there. That is what occurred to me when I recovered, at least; I am not sure now that it would have made any particular difference, and I am satisfied that it was better as it was. I returned to conscious-ness again, then, to find Bran and Captain Brague bending over me with solemn faces. I sat up and looked around me. I was sitting on a chair—for a moment my recollection hovered, and then I shook myself together and prepared to act. I was ashamed of my weak-ness, but it was over now, and though the whole thing was a horrid, a wretched bore, and really quite unjust, I knew that I had to see it through. I never had been wanting in resolu-tion, and now that I felt that I was in difficul-ties, I resolved to get out of them as soon as possible and with as much spirit as I could command. I waited for an instant, until I felt that I could speak with firmness and then I said—

"This is a very unfortunate affair."

"Yes," said Bran, with a deep breath. "It is."

Captain Brague began to protest that he was overwhelmed with grief—that he had taken me for some one else— I stopped him and bade him tell me as quickly as possible how he had come to follow me to the restaurant. I had a pretty correct idea of the truth, but I wanted to hear his story and I wanted Bran to hear it too. He began to falter a little, saying that he couldn't tell me the name of the person for whom he had mistaken me.

"I don't ask you for that," said I. "Be as quick as possible."

So he told us what had happened, as I have told it above. I noticed that Bran was darting glances of fury at him; and when he had finished, I made them promise solemnly that they would speak to nobody on the subject, not even to each other, until I asked them to do so. I sent Bran once more for a carriage, and took advantage of the opportunity thus offered for a little further reflection. I quickly decided to go back to my mother's; I preferred to run the chance of delaying an explanation with Penny rather than to take the risk of having a—well, a *row* at home. I knew that when Penny's temper was gone from him he wouldn't think of his surroundings, and I really could not bear the idea of furnishing material for kitchen gossip and scandal. Therefore, when Bran came back, I bade both the men good-night as politely as I could, smiling a little to myself as I perceived by their countenances that each had expected to be my prop and stay in my affliction, put myself in the carriage and drove to my mother's house. I had to ring her up, unfortunately; and when she came to the door she was in a mood to know why I wanted shelter with her.

" Mamma," said I, " I'll tell you in the morning."

" Ethel," she said, " you have had a quarrel with your husband."

Willful as I was, I was not utterly lacking in human kindness; so I sat down and told her the whole story. But I refused to take counsel with her that night, and I went to bed, pro-

visionally, for the day—"in order to wait de-
velopments," as the newspapers say,—declaring
that I was not to be disturbed for any body
less than my husband himself.   And during
that day I waited and reflected, expecting every
moment to hear Penny's voice in the hall below
me.   After that I came down-stairs and joined
my mother unto myself. · And by that time
matters had developed themselves with a vengeance.

My reflections had brought me to this conclusion : that the whole thing was a wretched
bore and that it was really not my fault—which
was, it will be observed, the point from which I
had started—that appearances were decidedly
against me, and that I owed it to my husband
to go to him and explain every thing and leave
the matter in his hands.   But to this course of
action an obstacle presented itself which rendered all my reflections of no avail—namely,
the fact that Penny had gone to Europe.

For the first time in my life I tasted the bitterness of despair.   Oh how wretched I was—

mentally and physically! If I could only have
arranged matters respectably with Penny—if I
could only have presented myself to the world
as a spouse at perfect accord with her husband
in spite of all that had passed—if I had only
been in a position to snub the weaklings and
defy the strong—for aught I would have cared
the whole story might have been sounded
throughout the length and breadth of the land
by brazen trumpets and published in the London *Truth* as well! But as things stood I was
at the mercy of every body in town. And it
would have been idle for me to suppose that
nobody knew what had happened. Of course
I had not spoken to any one. Bran Boullter
and Captain Brague had been equally silent, I
was quite sure, and all the indications pointed
to the conclusion that Penny had departed in a
fit of rage without taking any body into his confidence. But there is in society a breed of
pointers who are as quick to detect an incipient
scandal and as true to indicate its position as
ever is the thoroughbred to discover a covey.

Rumors flew about as thick as snowflakes; some were absurd and none were absolutely correct—but all connected the break between Penny and myself with the Maennerchor, and most of them of course brought in poor Captain Brague. And the real culprit all the time was Emma Maples! It was too aggravating! "A good chance for Mrs. Charter to keep Lent!" people cried—" she hasn't done such a thing for several years." Oh how furious it made me to think how all the idle old heads were bobbing and the false old fronts bristling, and the venomous old tongues wagging! And really my condition of mind might well have been desperate. I was ready to do any thing—I would have been obliged to any body for any good practical suggestion—but really there was nothing to be done. My real friends were very good to me, however. They came to see me. Lotty the first—she, dear girl, came on the instant, and insisted on full confidence, and gave me counsel out of her own heart and never once told me what Mason said. Olive came, too, and Miss Mayburn. They gave me my own time, never alluding to the unfortunate state of affairs. At first I could not talk it over with them. I wanted action, as I say, and Lotty and my mother were alone in my confidence. I don't know what Bran thought. I dare say he blamed himself terribly and was tortured by remorse—but I can't say I thought much about him at the time. He sent me a card the day after the little affair with—" Forgive me, and remember that I am at your service—" written on it. But I tore it up impatiently and threw it into the fire, wondering what good he thought he could do. Captain Brague must have been broken-hearted. I know that Katty Langton, bless his good soul, was, to use his own phrase, "infernally broken up about it," and instantly framed a hundred wild plans for helping me, which the superior good sense of Paddy Gander alone prevented him from putting into execution.

But when I think of the behavior of Emma Maples! Of course she must have known

what had happened, though I don't believe
Captain Brague told her any thing directly.
She knew that I had found out that it was for
her that the captain had mistaken me—of that
I am certain; but she never once came near
me! Never did she bring me the company
that misery loves; never—looking at it in the
most petty light—did she attempt to gratify
that foolish little desire that I felt, that every
one feels—the desire to talk it all over with
some one who had had a hand in it—her
wretched selfishness bred in her a mean cowardice and a pitiful fear that I would work on
her feelings and make her tell my husband that
it was her fault! Goodness! She was inex-
pressibly mean! At any rate—how degrading
it is to speak of it!—she need only have given
Penny the merest hint, the slightest word; and
as for thinking that I would have descended to
asking her to do it—! I grant that she did not
have much opportunity to show her generosity;
but she did have *one* opportunity, from the em-
bracing of which she fled in wild alarm. But

I degrade myself by speaking of her. And really I am not generally so violent; but cowardice I cannot excuse, and, whatever may have been my faults I never have been mean.

Such an outcry as the above, moreover, I have never made before. I was forced at the time to eat my sorrows and to drink my tears. I would not, above all things, have told my mother any thing about Emma Maples, for she was, I am sorry to say, in a somewhat vindictive temper. Her advice—in the first transports of her disappointment—was recrimination and she offered to supply me with much artillery in the shape of well-defined misbehavings on the part of my husband. Not that she actually had it on hand—but she proposed to discover it. It must be remembered, however, in her credit, that she was in a state of despair, for her whole gorgeous temple had been pulled down about her ears. And then she was of a much more fiery and energetic temperament than I was, even when roused. I hope it is unnecessary for me to say that I never listened

to her advice. Such a proceeding would have
been utterly foreign to my nature; and though
inaction was weighing terribly upon me it was
really for a definite understanding on the subject of my position that I longed rather than
for the active process of separation or recon-
cilement. But I subdued myself, and, at the
end of three or four weeks, knowing that people
generally had ceased to talk about the matter,
I took as dignified a stand as I could, went to a
few places and showed myself bravely, straight-
ened my back and held my head up, and only
wore a more scornful smile and a more defiant
air when that soulless old harridan, Mrs. Poti-
phar, dared to cut me on Walnut street.

But oh, what a blow it was! All that made
life dear to me had been rudely snatched away
from me. I was worse than undone. Could I
see nothing before me but a tiresome progress
upwards towards a meager position among the
second-rates? The thought was sickening!
Well, I will not weary the reader by dwelling
upon the unhappy feelings which beset me.

Little would any sympathizing soul care to hear of my sister, who came from Lancaster with, "I told you so!" written in letters of living fire on a hypocritical forehead and a malicious gleam in a subdued eye ; and less, I hope, would any body care to hear of her admirable husband, who comforted me by pointing out the opportunities which would be offered to me by the laws of the Commonwealth if Mr. Charter prolonged his stay in Europe for a specified period. It is sufficient to say that my cross was hard to bear, and that in the course of two or three months, what with my cares and the strain on my system, and, I am inclined to think, the improved methods of drainage provided for us by the officials who are the result of a popular system of government, I fell ill of a typhoid and became very low indeed.

It was Middleton Hall who brought my husband and myself together again—a strange ironical decree of Fate. I deserved it of him less than of any body else—far less than of Bran Boullter, for Bran was scarcely clear of

blame. Mr. Hall and my husband met in Heidelberg, where the former had been for several
years. What impulse prompted Penny to con-
fide in him, I cannot say. Penny's sudden resolu-
tion to go abroad was comprehensible enough.
He has told me that his first idea was to turn
the city upside down, and that he was only de-
terred from doing this by the reflection that a
certain editor of a Sunday newspaper whom he
had once caused to be put off a race-course
would then have a beautiful chance for revenge.
So it was natural, as I say, that he should conclude that the only safe way to keep himself
from making an awful explosion was to be off.
But at the time when he met Mr. Hall he was
beginning to feel quite free of the whole affair;
so I think I have to thank Providence and
Providence alone for making him take counsel
with a man so fitted to advise and so honorable
of judgment. The news of my illness had not
yet reached him, and possibly he might never
have heard of it in time, for no one knew his
whereabouts; it was Mr. Hall's grave and dig-

nified advice (warmed by the feelings which I am afraid he still cherished towards. me) that made Penny return home to find me unconscious, and, as every one thought, dying. So it happened that when I returned to life for a while I found him by my side ; and, knowing then that I had all that I had feared I had lost, I determined to get well—and I did. But when I recovered I was a different woman. The long days of my convalescence, the *petits soins* of my husband, the cheerful presence of Lotty (and her baby). and the earnest words of Olive and Miss Mayburn had their effect upon me. I don't mean to say that I became emotional. The leopard cannot change his spots, nor the Ethiop his skin, and I have always preserved a great contempt for emotion as a rule of life.

Penny took me to our own house as soon as possible, and there, leaning back comfortably in an easy chair in the bay window where I usually spent the morning, where the sunbeams could make more rosy my pale hands and glint across the delicate blue folds of my chamber gown, I mused over my life, wrought out my repentance, and planned my reform. "Life," I said to myself, "is a troubled sea, and the only compass for the barks that sail upon it is the compass of Duty." This commonplace is only commonplace because it is so very true.

And what, then, are the duties of married women? I remember that once, in the course of a conversation about the progress of human ideas which I had with Middleton Hall during the early days of our acquaintance, he told me that the movement of civilization was "from Status to Contract." I never wholly understood this phrase, but I have a fair idea of its meaning and I know what is meant by saying that the idea of the contract is the idea of modern civilization.

If women are no longer the handmaids they are the partners of their husbands; they enter into contracts with them; they owe duties to them and through them to society, which they must pay. For we all must contract to assist each other; if we did not owe to each other toleration, support and protection, modern society would tumble to pieces. Society must exist; if you imperil its existence by refusing to agree to its requirements it will crush you. The people at whom I laughed in Newport were quite right, after all. There was no reason why they should have been tolerant towards a woman who rode over and trampled down their moral flower-gardens,—especially as they knew that they had planted no seeds and used no gardening implements but those advertised and supplied by society. Their remonstrances were perfectly proper; and if ever I meet any of them again I shall be tempted to tell them so.

I hope that my moral is easy to understand.

Girls, be careful! Do not be led away by your desires for racketing amusements and careless enjoyment. You cannot take your lives into your own hands and defy society! You cannot live according to your own sweet wills! If you endeavor to do so your ideas will become more and more relaxed, and you will wind up with a big smash, just as I did. Observe, I say to you again, observe the rules which society prescribes. They may be different in Ashantee from what they are here—if you choose to go and live in Ashantee you need not conform to our notions—but they always exist and insensibly make themselves felt. They are always suited to the genius of the people among which they are found, and you must follow and not try to lead, unless you feel yourself inspired. But then the inspiration must be direct —for nobody can afford to make a mistake about inspiration.

If I had known the wisdom which I now possess a little earlier, I might have avoided all my errors and married Middleton Hall; and I should not have been forced to wait,—as I am now forced to wait—before taking the absolute lead in society as far as in me lies. For as the emblems of authority are the necessaries of a man's existence, so are position and conse-

quence the base and the only solid foundation
for the existence of a woman. But in course
of time this for which I wait shall come to me.
I will be an arbitress, a judge ; and my example
shall be that of a woman who does her duty.
If I am mistaken in this—as I do not think I
am likely to be—I will change my theories yet
once more and believe that woman is a domestic
animal. I will sit by the fire, purr, drink tea,
and knit stockings.

And if I had married Middleton Hall, how
entirely satisfactory my life would have been.
The wife of a man of splendid dignity and reputation, I could have assumed the position of a
leader in society in a far higher sense than
simply that of a popular belle, a gay priestess
of feasts and follies. My chosen acquaintances
would have been honorable, educated, literary.
I should have had foolish intimacies with nobody, and frivolity would have been beneath
me. I should have maintained a *salon*, and not
even my husband should always have shared
my inmost confidence. But that cannot be.

I have chosen for better for worse. I recognize that fact, and can fairly say that I am happy. As for emotional or hysterical moods, I have none. I am long past the time, and I can smile at the recollection of it, when I could dwell with pleasure on the Arcadian ideal of love in a cottage. My life is practical, and I am glad to think that I do not rest upon the counsels of any *directeur*, lay or spiritual. Of course I do not mean to give the impression that I have not awakened to a sense of my duties in regard to religion. I know now that for a long time I was a very godless woman. I go to church; I take a just interest in parish work; I am a directress of one hospital and a visitor to another. In a word, I know that religion is one of my duties—the highest of them—and I am persuaded that I have to the best of my ability thought over the whole circle of my duties, religion among them, and give to each its proper share of attention.

I have been deprived of one more advantage by my misfortunes. I see other women able to

indulge their finer feelings in their associations
with their families, their husbands, and their
children. I do not consider that such transports, such delights, come under the head of
what I have roughly condemned as emotional
absurdities. They are intellectual, they are
proper; they are the same feelings that one experiences on reading an exquisite piece of
tender description or witnessing a fine piece
of tragic acting. Yet they are denied to me.
From my family I have never been accustomed
to derive them—and as regards my husband,
though I may occupy the position that Mr.
Latitude suggested for me, that of a " repent-
ant spouse,"—it will be remembered that I
gave a hint in the first part of my story that
the result of my illness was to thin my hair and
ruin my complexion. Such was, indeed, the
melancholy fact. I regret it; it is perhaps my
deepest cause for regret; but it is irremediable,
except by nature. I only think of it in the
connection of which I am now speaking. It
has caused a diminution of my husband's

affection towards me. As he married me in a great measure on account of my beauty, and as I used it to make him marry me, I can scarcely complain; and, indeed, I think it rather hard on him. The fact remains, however, that the first rapture is over. I have no children, but perhaps I shall have them; and at all events I have the consolation of knowing that if I have not as much of my husband's affection as I once had, I have all his respect and confidence. And without that from her husband a woman is powerless, except to work on the feelings of credulous males; and that she ought to be ashamed to do.

THE END.